The Grandnan

For Pirate Stephen. AD
For my dad. Arrrr! SMK

BOING

PUFFIN BOOKS

UK | USA | Canada | Ireland | Australia
India | New Zealand | South Africa | China

Penguin Random House Australia is part of the Penguin Random House group of
companies whose addresses can be found at global.penguinrandomhouse.com.

Penguin
Random House
Australia

First published by Puffin Books, an imprint of
Penguin Random House Australia Pty Ltd, in 2019

Cover design by Stephen Michael King and Tony Palmer
© Penguin Random House Australia Pty Ltd
Text design by Tony Palmer © Penguin Random House Australia Pty Ltd
Typeset by Midland Typesetters, Australia

Printed and bound in Australia by Griffin Press, part of Ovato, an accredited
ISO AS/NZS 14001 Environmental Management Systems printer.

A catalogue record for this
book is available from the
National Library of Australia

ISBN 978 0 14 379654 1

Penguin Random House Australia uses papers that are natural and recyclable products,
made from wood grown in sustainable forests. The logging and manufacture processes
are expected to conform to the environmental regulations of the country of origin.

penguin.com.au

Atticus Van Tasticus

Andrew Daddo

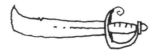

Stephen Michael King

Puffin Books

Magic Harry

Silent Type

Princess

THE CREW

Muscles

First Mate

Wrong Way Warren!

Two Times

Stinkeye

Fishface

Buttface

Mullet

Rod (Lightning Rod)

Slapfoot

Atticus

Hogbreath

~~Every single part of this story is historically correct, unless it's not.~~

~~This work of non-fiction is pretty much historically and factually correct~~

~~Some of this true story might be made up~~

~~None of this is true~~

~~This is rubbish~~

A story

Yay   Arrrrr

Prologue

All Legends
Start Somewhere

Atticus Van Tasticus was a pretty normal boy, from a fairly normal family, who just happened to have an abnormally wealthy grandnan. As in, she was stuffed with the stuff. 'More money than God,' as the saying goes.

I don't need money. I own the universe.

The way his family sucked up to Grandnan Van Tasticus drove Atticus completely bonkers, but he got it.

Whenever she was around, everyone was on their best manners. It was all, 'Yes, Grandnan. No, Grandnan. Can I've a fist full of gold, Grandnan?' She'd bat her eyes and pucker up, but never opened her purse.

Well, almost never. And the Van Tasticus family had tried everything.

It's not as if she wasn't generous.

Every grandkid got one shot at her riches: it was a family thing, like a tradition. Great-Grandnan Van Tasticus had given her

grandkids the exact same shot, and so had
Great-Great-Grandnan Van Tasticus.

And on it had gone for as
long as anyone could remember.

Here,
Fido

1,000,000 BC

Atticus's dad said it was stupid. 'This is
stupid,' he said. 'It's ridiculous. Most kids
would rather have a dress-ups costume
than some junky old painting that would
be worth thousands of dollars after the old
painter turned his toes up. Who would let
a ten-year-old choose their own destiny?'

The really stupid thing
was what he chose on his
tenth birthday.

Dad's choice

Atticus's mum said it was pathetic. 'This is pathetic,' she said. But only because her nan wasn't rich like Grandnan Van Tasticus and all the Grandnan Van Tasticuses before her.

Dame Van Tasticus I

Dame Van Tasticus II

Dame Van Tasticus III

Dame Van Tasticus IV

Mum's nan was from a very different line of grandmas.

Baking Nan

Cat loving Nan

Hot chocolate making Nan

Gardening Nan

Atticus knew his turn to choose was coming, and he had to get it right. His mum and dad reminded him all the time, and he couldn't stuff it up. The future lushness of his family depended on him, and him alone. He had one shot, and knew Grandnan would say something like, 'Use this to make something of yourself. To make the world a better place. Go forth and prosper. *Do what you wanna do, be what you wanna be – yeah*!'

His brother had blown it badly on his tenth birthday.

His sister hadn't done much better.

Aunty Agnes was a joke.

Uncle Edward was a fool.

And Dad, well. The less said about that the better.

Now it was up to Atticus.

Chapter 1

1750 or So

On the morning of the night before Atticus turned ten, his parents began the very big job of getting him ready.

'You are a grub,' said Mum, practically sanding him with soap.

'And the smell,' said Dad, tipping another bucket of cold water on him.

'Eeewwww!' they both shrieked.

Atticus couldn't believe it. He smelt good. He could smell his richness without even trying. It was a good honest smell, like a horse in the rain, or a dog fresh out of a puddle. And the dirt made his skin match the colour of his hair. He thought he was pretty much perfect.

He just wished he was strong
enough to wriggle free from the soap.

'Stop wriggling,' said his father.
'You have to be clean and fresh and brilliant,
so if you stuff up your choice, you'll get
another chance. Don't you see? Stay still so
we can help you.'

'It doesn't matter what I look like.' Atticus
squirmed. 'As Grandnan says, "You get what
you get and you don't get upset!".'

Atticus was scrubbed so clean he felt dirty.
Then he was pushed into tights and pulled
into a shirt. His hair was scraped across his
head and glued down tight, his teeth polished,
and his shoes were an ornament to Narcissus,
the God of reflection.

He stood in front of the mirror and
shuddered at the boy looking
back at him.

'Beautiful,' said his mother.
'Superb,' said his father.

Narcissus

8

Before   After

'Oh, please,' groaned Atticus.

He didn't look like himself at all. Normally
what he saw was a handsome young man
with a jaw that jutted out like a boulder at
the bottom of a granite cliff. Sharp, capable
cheeks leading to a ferocious brow to shield
his dark eyes and launch the thatch of hair on
his head the way an island sprouts palm trees.
With his shirt off and pants well hitched,
he was on the definitely side of awesome.
Best of all, there was a hair under his arm.
Just the one. Mum always wanted to pluck it,

but Atticus would say, 'No, Mother. It's my hair. You never know when I might need it.'

That Atticus was exactly nothing like the one in the mirror. This Atticus looked like a kid – it was embarrassing.

'Arrrrgh,' he went. 'If I have to stay like this a second longer than I have to, I'm going to lose my poop.'

'You look gorgeous, Atty,' said his mum, licking her hand and using the slobber to stick down some stray hairs. 'Just how Grandnan would want. In fact, you look so good, I bet if you make a silly choice she'll give you another go on this most special day of the Van Tasticus family tradition.'

Chapter 2

The Tradition

The day you turn ten in the Van Tasticus house goes pretty much like this.

Grandnan's horse-drawn coach arrived and the freshly minted double-digiter begged to take the reins. The answer was always the same from the grumpy buffoon up front and every ten-year-old worth their salt grizzled and said, 'If I'm old enough to get to choose something – anything – from Grandnan Van Tasticus's giant shed, I'm old enough to whip your fat horse into a canter.'

No parents were allowed. Only the ten-year-old went to Grandnan's.

Through the gate, up the drive, past the giant woolly dogs and all the way to the steps in front of the house. The door creeeeeaked open, and that's where you found Grandnan Van Tasticus.

She probably wasn't as scary as she looked, but Atticus still felt a bit like a little kid in a big kids' boxing match.

I'm not asking for the full Poodle, just a trim every now and again.

'Hello, Grandnan,' he said, puckering up like he meant it.

Hello, Grandnan

'Aaaaaatticus, the last of my ten-year-olds.' She smiled, offering a cheek to his lips. 'You ready?'

Mwah!

'Mmm hmmm,' he said, still pretty shaky.

'You sure?'

'Think so.'

'You know the deal?'

'Mmmmm hmmmm,' he said again. He really didn't trust himself to speak.

'Let me remind you, just in case: You can go into my old shed and choose anything you want. Anything. It's yours. Forever. To do with as you wish. You can use it. Or sell it. Or burn it. Whatever. There are things of great value and things worth less than nothing. But be careful, don't

look with your head, Atticus.
You're a good boy. Look with
your heart.'

Whilst you're in there,
can you grab me that
piano accordian?

Poppy Van Tasticus

It was the exact opposite
of what his mother and
father had told him. And
his brother and his sister
and his aunty and uncle, too.
They'd said, 'Choose with your head, you
idiot. Your heart's got no brains.'

Grandnan Van Tasticus took him by the
hand and walked him to the giant shed, where
two men the size of elephants waited.

'Open it up,' she said to them.

They heaved and hauled and struggled
with the giant doors.

'You should put these doors on wheels
or rollers,' whispered Atticus. 'Then they'd be
roller doors.'

Grandnan patted his head in the nicest
possible way then pointed towards a massive

building. It was hardly a shed like he'd expected – more like a museum.

'Your heart, Atticus Van Tasticus. Choose one thing with your heart. You have all day, so there is no rush. But be certain – you only get one chance, it's a forever pick.'

His heart was practically beating out of his chest. If not for his puffy shirt, she'd have seen it for sure. With the doors all the way open, what Atticus saw looked like paradise. A bounty like you'd only ever imagined. There was hoards of stuff, it must have taken her ages to collect it all. Was that unicorn alive or stuffed? Was that a locked treasure chest? He could see cupboards overflowing with clothes and carpets and beautiful rugs. The walls were lined with paintings, and there were more on the floor.

Atticus's heart soared. It heaved and thumped and jumped, and he put his hand on so many things as the words

formed in his mouth. 'This is the one!' he wanted to say, over and over.

Grandnan followed along, but never said a word. And Atticus didn't utter more than a series of delighted grunts.

He ventured deeper, past the stuffed woolly mammoth, to where things got dusty. He could feel he was close. But as hard as he looked, nothing took his

breath away. Not the giant
grandfather clock or the

heavy bag on the ground with 'gold'
stamped on it. *Fake*, he thought. *Has to be fake.*
Not the funny looking thing that might one
day be called a bike. Not even the enormous
man-sized basket attached to ropes which
were attached to a giant balloon waiting to
be blown up.

Atticus sighed when he hit the back wall
of the shed.

He'd missed it, and he'd been in there
for ages.

There was pretty much nothing else to see.

But then Atticus looked into the gloom and
saw a crown full of jewels and remembered
the words from his parents. 'Use your head,
Atticus. Use your head.' *Could it be the crown?*

He looked at his grandnan, who
was halfway to filthy, and she raised one
eyebrow. It had to be the crown, didn't it?
Out here where the dust was deep. *It was
a trick of Grandnan to have the best stuff way
out back*, Atticus thought. She knew he
wouldn't be able to wait to pick something
early on in the quest. She knew he'd grab
something from the front like the others
always did. He was ten and impatient. They all
were. How would they be able to hold out for
the good stuff hidden under a layer of filth
out the back if she loaded the fun stuff at
the front?

Atticus picked up the crown, took a huge gulp of air and blew as hard as he could. It was most definitely beautiful. He took a second breath, ready for a bigger blow but sneezed like he had a hurricane inside him.

Achoooooooooooooeeeewwww!

He sneezed so hard he sneezed himself into a somersault and rolled through a small wooden trapdoor into a dark, wooden room. His heart skipped a beat.

He'd found it, he was sure.

'I want this,' he said, fumbling for the crown. 'Grandnan, I CHOOSE THIS!'

'The crown?' she puffed once she'd arrived. Grandnan Van Tasticus might have sounded the tiniest bit disappointed. 'That old thing? Why? Do you think you're going to be a king?'

BOING

That's it!

Atticus shook his head and passed the crown to Grandnan. 'Not that junky thing,' he said. With his arms wide, he smiled. 'This!'

His heart said it was right.

Grandnan took a step back, looking into the gloom, hoping to see what Atticus saw. She took another step back, then another and another until, finally, she could see the whole thing. It was huge, so big you couldn't see it from up close.

'Oh, I'd forgotten about that,' she said, the smile back in her voice. 'What are you going to do with that?'

'Well, der, Grandnan. I'm going to be a pirate!'

Chapter 3

Captain Van Tasticus

When Atticus thought about it, the only thing that came even close to pirating was running off to the circus. But what if he had to bunk in with the bearded lady? What if the clowns got hold of him? What if he grew too fast and they needed an extra dwarf to fire out of a cannon so they chopped his shins off and stuck his feet to the bottom of his knees? What if there was a goat shortage and they needed food for the lions? What if, what if, what if?

Much better to be a pirate, he figured. What could possibly go wrong with that?

Besides, Grandnan seemed to be into it. She hauled Atticus into a bossomy hug and whispered, 'It's as spirited a choice as anyone's ever made in the long, long history of the Van Tasticuses. It's fantastic, Atticus Van Tasticus. A bit like you.'

In fact, Grandnan was so happy with his choice, she even let him into the house. Just about no one was allowed in there, not even

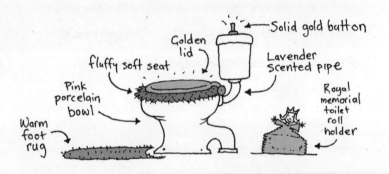

Golden lid

Solid gold button

fluffy soft seat

Lavender scented pipe

Pink porcelain bowl

Royal memorial toilet roll holder

Warm foot rug

to pee or poop. Then, after a quick tour and a long wash, she set him free in the sewing room with a bag of material scraps and a cool, black bedsheet. 'You're going to need a flag, boyo.'

By the end of the day he was ready.

Chapter 4

Onwards

Saying goodbye to Grandnan was harder than Atticus had expected. She got him into a hug and squeezed him so hard he thought he'd pop. *Like my big brother's zits*, he thought. *She's going to pop me like a zit!*

Big brother
Dave VanTasticus

Pimples bigger
than eyes

But she didn't, not even close. It was nice, like being crushed in a big, pillowy headlock. And best of all, she offered Atticus a loan

of her big strong friends, Hulk and Hogan, to help get his brand-new-to-him ship to the ocean. If Atticus was honest, he had been wondering how he might shift it. He'd even poked around a bit to see if there was something he could use.

He looked at the ass and wondered if he could use that. Being a cross between a horse and a donkey, it could be strong enough if he could balance his ship on its back. Then he saw the cart the beast was usually attached to, and he tried to imagine his pirate ship in there. It was nuts to even think of it.

But what about two carts and two asses?

Or three carts in a row, and a whole bunch of asses lined up together. On the road.

Eee yore)

Translates to:
'Hey! I'm no sacrificial lamb — more like a sacred cow.'

In a line, maybe in pairs, all hitched together ready to work as a team. Wow. It could work.

It should work.

He never got the chance to find out. Hulk and Hogan pushed his thoughts aside and said they'd get the ship to the docks. It wasn't easy, but not nearly as hard as he thought. Between grunts and groans and swearing and pushing, Hogan and Hulk told Atticus that before they worked for Grandnan and became her special friends, they'd done a bunch of other things. They'd been wrestlers. Coal miners. Actors. Lute players. Landlubbers and removalists.

They had ideas on how to move pretty
much anything, including Atticus's ship.

Log over log over log, they pushed it.

Log over log, his beautiful pirate ship
rolled. Across the day and through the night
and through another day, past all sorts of
people and animals and even a person
dressed as an animal – or maybe that was
the other way round.

All the way to the seaside.

Something I picked up in Southern Europe.

Something I picked up in Scotland.

Plunk plankity plunk

Atticus fed and watered Hulk and Hogan
from Grandnan's giant lunch box, gave
directions and warned them if they were
going to run into anything. If it hadn't
been for Atticus, Drunk Diablo would
have been flattened a bunch of times.
Splat, flat, no more of that.

Chapter 5

Seaside

Up until they got to the seaside, everything went swimmingly, pretty much. There was that one thing that everyone swore they'd never talk about, and they stuck to their word. But apart from that, the big move was peachy.

It was when they got to the seaside that things got funky.

Lots of little things happened, but there were two big things. Somehow, there was a hole in the boat no one could remember seeing or making. That led to the second problem: how to fix the hole. Hogan and Hulk had been lots of things, but hole-fixers wasn't one of them.

I sewed a button on once

and I've cooked a stew

but we've never fixed a hole.

Atticus had no history of fixing holes, either. But if he knew one thing, it was that to fix a hole, you had to be able to get to it. Maybe worst of all, this hole was right on the bottom of the boat.

'Hulk, Hogan, we have a problem,' said Atticus, looking down at the docks. There were people everywhere. Ships, boats, sails hanging up to dry. If you can imagine

A pillow slip
(filled with goose feather)

A silk slip
(with French Bow)

A boat slip
(A wet parking space)

anything to do with a shipyard, it was there, laid out in front of them in full glorious brown, the colour of pretty much everything back in the day.

The only thing they couldn't see was a spare slip for Atticus's ship so they could fix the hole. Not one slip for his ship. Not one spot to fix Atticus's holey boat. He cursed, regretting it instantly. The big guy above would not be impressed. Surely a holy boat would be better than a holey boat.

Hogan and Hulk took the chance to rest while Atticus considered his options. He made a list.

1. Wait.
2. Push someone's boat out of a slip.
3. Make his own slip at the end of the cove.
4. Make a whole new marina, first for his ship, then for other people who wouldn't fit in this one. If it was good, he could abandon the idea of pirating and become a marina owner and be richer than God.
5. Apologise for cursing, again.
6. Forget option 4 because 'I really want to be a pirate'.
7. Find another way.

A little sad, he walked down into the cove and asked how long people were expecting to be in the slips for. They had all the answers, but none of the right ones.

'Ages.'

'Forever.'

'Yonks.'

'Yonks?'

'Yeah, yonks! Ages! Yonks are ages,

I've been here as long as I can remember.

ya daft punk! Why? In a hurry, are ya? Goin'
somewhere, are ya? Got somewhere to be,
have ya? Have ya? Got somewhere to be?'
He barely looked at Atticus, looking around
at everything else while he bellowed.

Atticus looked to the grump and held
his tongue.

'Oh, gone quiet, have ya? Quiet one, is ya?

WE'S GOT A QUIET ONE 'ERE, LADS!'

he roared to no one in particular.

'HE'S GOT THE QUIETS, HE HAS!

Haven't ya? Haven't ya?'

Atticus shook his head the tiniest bit and whispered, 'No,' like he wasn't sure.

'Oh, aye. A mouthy one, is ya? A mouthy one.'

As Atticus turned and walked away, he didn't utter another sound.

'AND RUDE. AND RUDE!'

yelled the man. 'Too good to talk to me, eh? A rude, quiet, mouthy one. Now I've seen everything and it's not yet midday!'

Atticus pulled the list out of his pocket
and added:

8. Avoid LOUD Hairy men

who love the sound of their own voices.

Out of shouting distance, he stood on
his toes and had another look around. There
was one last spot, right down the end of the
cove near the flatlands – down where the
manky boats were. Hulk and Hogan followed
his gaze and saw it too. Without being asked,
they re-aligned their logs and set forth for the
end spot. Given it was mostly downhill, they
managed it quickly.

It was about as much fun as they'd ever
had. Atticus added this new idea to his list.

Roll and then coast, then coast and roll.
A coaster-roller.

In his head, he could see it, clear as anything. Fashion a special track where you could ride up and down and it would feel dangerous and thrilling and great for parents and kids and they'd come from everywhere to ride it, especially a seaside spot like this.

9. Make a track to the seaside and roll carts down it so they go fast enough to SCARE but not kill you...

Then he thought, *If I do that, I won't be piratin'*. So he banked the idea for another day.

He had a better look at the land around him. He'd been wrong.

There was no easy way to fix his boat. And he knew they'd never get it back up the hills they'd just coaster-rollered down; they were just too steep. It was either fix his ship, or abandon his dream altogether.

Atticus thought. 'The hole's in the bottom, right?' he said to Hulk and Hogan, who nodded. 'So our options are . . .'

Chapter 6

Swingin' Ships

Hulk and Hogan folded their massive arms and rubbed their chins.

'We could go for a little careening. You know, roll the ship on its side to get to the hole like that. But there's not really enough room. Maybe what we need to do is . . .' started Atticus.

The giants nodded their heads, their eyebrows were up in an expectant kind of way.

'. . . get it off the ground, for one,' said Atticus. 'Then we can get to the hole and fix it. Can you hold it off the ground while I do that?'

'It's pretty heavy,' said Hulk.

'And bulky,' said Hogan.

'We could try,' they said together. 'But if we dropped it, you'd be flat, as in splat.'

'Buuuuuuut,' said Hogan, 'we could build a frame with those big logs and use that rope to hold it and then we could –' He stopped talking and started gesturing, which made Hulk start talking and pointing.

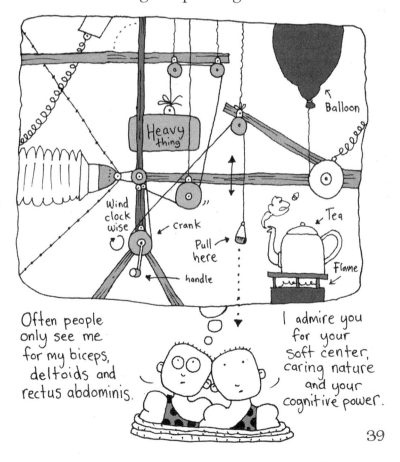

Before Atticus knew it, they were off and at it. There was sawing and banging and hammering and yammering and, after erupting out of a cloud of dust and smoke, they were done.

Finished.

It was amazing, like nothing Atticus'd ever seen.

Hulk and Hogan could barely wipe the grins off their massive faces as they tied the final knots on their creation. 'If we tug on this, the ship'll go up. We can push the bow end to make it move a bit. Or the stern end. Once it's where you want, we can hold it in place. Okay, Atticus? Reckon it'll work?'

Atticus stood back and clapped his hands. Happy didn't cover it, not even close.

He grabbed the ladder and climbed aboard. 'Maybe. It looks pretty good – like, it could be genius,' he said. 'We'll be able to swing the ship to get it into just the right position, then

tie it off. We can fix the hole, we can paint and re-rope and all sorts of things with it sitting in this swing-thing. It's completely genius! Well done, Hulk and Hogan. It's perfect. And kind of like a swing. A giant Pirate Ship Swing. Will you push me?' Atticus was standing in the bow of the ship. 'Let's see if it works.'

Hulk and Hogan were careful at first, but after Atticus convinced them that it was actually quite fun, they got their backs into it.

'Higher!' he hollered. 'Higher!' The twins were into it, pushing one way, pulling the other. The ship was swinging back and forth, creaking a bit, but it was all good. People noticed what was going on from further up the shipyards and came to watch.

It was such fun, Atticus could barely stop laughing.

Once a crowd gathered round, Hulk and Hogan got self-conscious and stopped pushing. The ship gently swung to a stop.

The loud Grumpy Bum pushed through the throng and barked, 'Havin' a laugh, are ya? 'Avin' a good time, like? It looks like a good time. I like a good time. I'm a good time kind

of guy, I am.' He pointed at the ship in the
harness. 'Can I've a go? I'd like a laugh on
a thing like that, I would. I would.'

Then lots of other people asked for a go,
too. *A go?* thought Atticus. *A go? It's not a ride.
Or is it? Maybe it is. Like a carousel, only better.*

— Can I have a go?

⌣ Me too?

⌣ Please?

'No rides,' said Hulk. 'It's a ship.
We're fixing it.'

If you CURSE
one more time
you'll be
waiting
for eternity. ⌣

So
RUDE
you are.
)

'I'll pay ya, give you money and all that.
Just a quick go. Not a long one. Haven't had
a swing in years. Years!' said the Grump.
His face was quite different now that he was
smiling. He looked almost nice. Rotten teeth,
though. Really awful.

'I'll pay, too,' said someone else.
'And me, and me. And me. And me.'

They came from all over
the place.

'I can't pay but I can let
you pat me puppies,' said one old woman.

Atticus looked a little nervous, then
laughed. 'I hate to tell you, old toothless lady,
but they're not puppies. They're just little
dogs. But all right,' he said. 'On you go.'

Atticus took the money and held the dogs
while Hulk and Hogan helped everyone up
the ladder, loading them to the left and right
until the deck was packed. Hulk went aft,
Hogan went fore, and whilst Atticus cheered,
they pushed.

'Blu

'Woooooooh,' went the crowd on the little swings.

'Weeeeeeee,' they wailed as it got higher.

'Eeeeeeeeek,' they screamed, when it looked like doing a loop.

'S†ooooooop'

yelled the people.

'yuurgh'

spewed Drunk Diablo – all over everyone.

Why are there always carrots in it?

'Stoooooop!'

Grumpy Bum was steaming. And white. He would have been next to spew. 'This is a disgrace. A disgrace. Disgraceful. Awful. Dismantle this thing. It's dangerous. Dangerous, I say!'

Atticus said they'd made the sling to fix their boat. It wasn't meant to be a ride. Grumpy Bum was the one who'd wanted to ride it in the first place.

'Bahhh! Get rid of it! Rid of it! Baaaaah!' went Grumpy Bum.

Which they did, but not until most of the work was done. Atticus couldn't imagine anyone would want to ride in it again, anyway.

Nail

The last job was to make a stand for the ship so they could rest it there until the tide came in. Hogan and Hulk worried it could fall off the stand, so, when Atticus was otherwise occupied, they nailed it to the bottom of the ship.

They'd just have to remember to un-nail it before it was time to set sail.

Chapter 7

Clear the Decks

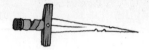

The water worked its way up the flatlands faster than Hulk and Hogan had expected. Much faster.

In good news, the ship stayed on its special stand, even when it was completely under water. Once the tide was all the way in, his beautiful ship gently rose and began to drift.

Working together with long poles, Hulk and Hogan guided her from the shallows to deeper water. Atticus ran below and searched

for leaks. It all looked pretty good. Dry,
certainly. And clean. There was room for
provisions and a crew, and now that he had
his pockets stuffed with cash
from the ride, he'd be able
to get organised and start
pirating.

Leak repair

Bandaid   Blob of tar

← Chewing
gum

They pushed the ship all
the way to the busiest part
of the docks, where Atticus
thanked Hulk and Hogan,
asking if they might come with him.

'Hulk. Hogan. Aarrrrrr! You two want
to come a piratin'?'

The two giants shared a look and shook
their heads.

Things that landlubbers need to consider
before choosing a life of pirating.

losing
both eyes

Losing
both arms

Having a
peg leg

Losing your
head

'Someone's got to keep an eye on your
grandnan, Atty. That's an excitin' enough
life for the likes of us.'

Atticus must have looked a bit broken,
because quick as a flash, Hulk added,

'We like the cut of your jib, lad. If you need us, another time, we might be able to help out.'

'We will be able to help out,' said Hogan. 'Deffo!'

They shook hands and bid each other farewell.

As Atticus watched them walk the plank to the pier, he noticed something else.

Someone on the docks, not much different to him but dirtier. As in, filthy, with long, straggly hair. There was a sign around the neck that said, 'Mate for hire.' The kid looked all right to Atticus. Perfect, actually.

His first thought was, *We could be mates. In fact, that kid could be my first mate.*

Chapter 8

The Crew

No dawdle, no fuss.

Atticus sang out that he was looking for a crew, and the grubby kid fairly leapt at it.

'So, meandyou, is it?'

Atticus had to slow the words down in his own head before he got what the boy meant.

'Yes,' nodded Atticus. 'Just me and you, so far.'

'So I's first, am I?' The kid looked strong enough, tall enough. Just in need of a wash, and maybe a haircut.

'That you are.'

'Aye, mate,' the kid said, beaming back at Atticus. 'Your first, mate.'

'First Mate,' repeated Atticus, thinking there was a ring to it. 'A captain needs a mate, and you're the first one I've found. Mate.'

'Proud to be your first mate, Cap'n. Call me, Mate.'

'Aye aye, Mate. First Mate.' Atticus smiled, pushing out his hand. 'Now, before we go piratin', we need the rest of the crew.'

'Where'd they be, Cap'n?'

'Not sure, Mate.'

'Have you lost 'em?' First Mate looked a little puzzled.

'Haven't found them, Mate.'

'Because they're lost, Cap'n?'

'Only because I'm looking for them, and they don't know they're yet to be found.'

Mate squinted his right eye at Atticus before saying, 'You're a deep thinkin' Cap'n. I like that.'

'That's good.' Atticus squinted back. 'Now, Mate, help me find my crew so we can get off this wharf and get piratin'.'

First Mate switched eyes, squinting with his left. 'Will yer tell me what they look like?'

Atticus looked off into the distance, somewhere between the sky and the horizon. 'They'll look like they want to be somewhere else, Mate. Somewhere fine, where the wind blows your hair back and the sun bakes your wet skin dry. A place of adventure and beauty and danger, where any minute could be your last, and your next minute might be your best.'

He looked back to First Mate. 'You'll know them when you see them.'

The penny dropped for First Mate as he realised there was no crew yet. Their job was to find one. From scratch. 'Is it boys or girls mainly? Do you care?' First Mate asked, but Atticus was off and searching already. 'I don't care,' First Mate said to no one. 'Makes no difference to me.'

Mate went in the opposite direction. They searched in alleys and windows and doorways, even under bridges. One boy was covered in paint, one in bites. They found a girl hauling a cart with the biggest upside-down smile ever,

and another pushing a pram like she wanted to let it run away from her – with the screaming baby inside it!

Wahhhhh

Kids who were kind of like them but of all shapes and sizes. After some pushing and pulling, they were lined up on the dock in front of the ship. These kids looked like they were from everywhere and nowhere at the same time.

'Look at yers!' barked First Mate. 'Standtallwouldya! It's time to salute ya Cap'n.'

Atticus walked forwards, shoulders back, chest out, chin thrust to an impossibly proud angle. 'There'll be no saluting, First Mate. We are more a team than a crew. Together we will work. Together we will sail. Together we're goin' piratin'. Everyone give me an *aarrrrrr*!'

'Errr!'

they went, only there wasn't much in it. It was probably more *ugh* than *aarrrrrr*!

First Mate was on to them. 'Come on, you mob. Give the Cap'n a proper *aarrrrr*!'

'Aargh?'

they went.

'No, AAARRR! AAARRR!'

There was lots of looking around and embarrassed smiles.

'Aargh? Aargh?'

'Don't worry about it, Mate,' said Atticus. 'There's time to work on the *aarrrrr*. Any chance of a *me hearties*?' They looked back at him blankly. 'All right, who are you, then? Sound off so we can get to know each other before we hit the high seas.'

But not a sound was uttered.

'Speak up.' First Mate did his best to bluster them into voice, but still no one coughed up more than a splutter. 'Don't make me give you names. I'll do it, I will. My names stick!'

'Warren,' came the smallest voice from the biggest boy. 'I'm Warren.'

'It's a start, Cap'n. We've got a Warren. Not quite what I was expecting, I'll say that. Anyone else? Can we get more than a "Warren"?'

But there was nothing. First Mate took a step back and folded his arms impatiently. 'Fine. Here goes.' He started at one end of the crew and pointed to each person as he said a name. 'Two Times. Stinkeye. Hogbreath. Slapfoot. Fishface. Mullet. Lightnin' Rod, Buttface. Magic Harry. Muscles . . .

Why call me Fishface?

And you. You will be . . . You will be . . .'

She was second to last in the line, the girl who'd been pushing the pram. 'You will be –'

'Princess,' said the girl next to her, the muscly one with the new name, Muscles. 'She's a princess.'

'I'm not.'

'You are now, Princess.'

'And what about you, there?' First Mate said to the one last in line, a brooding fellow who'd not uttered a sound. 'Any ideas on what you'd like to be called?'

The quiet one shrugged as if he wasn't fussed.

'Well, there must be somethin' we can call you,' First Mate badgered.

The boy frowned at First Mate, shrugged again, waved his hands and turned down the corners of his mouth.

'Anythin'?' tried First Mate, thinking he'd probably like to get off on the right foot with this one. But the kid said nothing, just offered a gesture that made First Mate suspect he was thinking a lot more than he was saying.

'Oh, I get it. The silent type. That's what we've got here, Cap'n. Seen this type before – he's either a very deep thinker, or not much of a thinker at all. We'll find out soon enough. He'll be good for somethin', that's for sure. Well, we can't stand here all day. On board, crew. Let's go piratin'! Arrrrrr!' went First Mate.

Everyone crossed the plank onto the ship. Everyone except Warren, who was walking the other way.

'Wrong way, Warren,' yelled First Mate. 'You're going the wrong way.'

Warren turned. 'I hear that a lot,' he said with a shrug.

'Then you shall be Wrong Way Warren,' laughed Atticus as he crossed the plank onto the ship.

64

'Welcome aboard, my crew. This is *The Grandnan*. The newest, bestest, most brilliant piratin' ship on these six seas.'

'Seven.'

'Seven,' said Princess. 'I think you'll find it's seven seas.'

Chapter 9

Away, Haul Away!

After the pushing off, and the scratching of heads, then pushing harder and some really hard scratching of heads, Muscles untied the ropes and they pushed off properly.

That's when things got real aboard *The Grandnan*.

To this point, it'd all been a bit of a lark

for Atticus, because even though he had a
boat that he was pretty sure would float, he
hadn't actually expected to go anywhere.

He'd figured his parents would stop him.

He'd figured Grandnan would ask for her
ship back.

He'd figured someone would ruin his fun
because, eventually, it's what happens to kids
just as things get really, really interesting.

Besides, who gives a kid a ship? What kind of
parent lets their son sail off in a ship they've
been given, anyway? And who'd let their kids

sail off in a ship full of other kids like it was normal. It was nuts.

Atticus didn't even know how to sail. Not really. He kind of knew what he was meant to say – he'd flicked through a couple of piratin' books, he'd hung around the docks and listened to the banter – but he was so overcome with excitement he couldn't remember a thing. Nothing but 'landlubber' and 'That's not a knife!'.

Let me. Let me.

I'd make a better pirate.

Let me run the show.

He knew the crew were waiting, so very quietly he mumbled, 'That's not a knife, you landlubber.' It was so quiet, First Mate almost missed it.

First Mate squinted hard at his captain with pursed lips. 'What's that, Cap'n? Was that an order?'

'It was indeed, First Mate.' Atticus nodded slowly. 'Indeed it was.'

'AARRRRRRRR!' roared First Mate. 'You heard the Cap'n!'

'Er, no we didn't,' said Princess, looking at the others, who shook their heads. 'We didn't, did we?'

'Aarrrrrr. AARRRRR!' First Mate was turning purple. 'Hoist the sails, yer dogs! Secure that anchor, yer spineless slugs! Landlubbers, the lot of yers!' And when they didn't move fast enough, he let go his biggest

This rope has to do something.

It's called a stay.

Grrrrr.

AAAAA AAARRR!

Stay where?

Everyone moved. The anchor was fastened so it didn't slap about against the hull, the sails

69

were hoisted and the crew did their bit, except for Warren, who instead of going up the mast, headed for the galley.

'Wrong Way Warren!' barked First Mate. 'That's the wrong way!'

'Sorry,' said Warren, pointing the right way. 'That way?'

And just like that – well, not really, but pretty much just like that – they were sailing. It was exactly as Atticus had imagined it.

'Plan, Cap'n?' asked First Mate.

'Good idea.' Atticus smiled. 'Your best one, yet.'

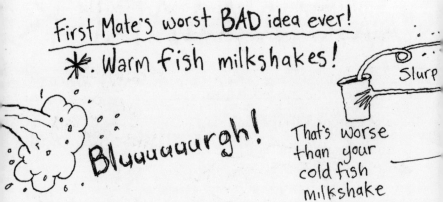

First Mate's worst BAD idea ever!
✳. Warm fish milkshakes!

Slurp

Bluuuuuurgh!

That's worse than your cold fish milkshake

Chapter 10

Living the Dream

Atticus took the wheel and looked around. If it was possible to be living the dream at the age of ten, this was surely it.

A gentle breeze filled the sails and the ship – *his* ship, his *pirate* ship – pushed forwards through the water with surprising ease, leaving a trail of foam and bubbles behind.

She was a beauty, her creaks and groans like a symphony.

And the players, his crew, even looked like they knew what they were doing.

I suggest
we go
that-a-way

First Mate stalked the deck, pointing and
barking like he'd done it all before.

'Swab the decks'

'polish the cannons'

'keep your eyes aft'

From Wrong Way Warren in the crow's
nest looking back to where they'd come from,
to Lightning Rod fooling about with the metal

spike off the front of the ship, everything looked perfect.

All that was missing was his Van Tasticus pirate flag waving from the flagpole. Atticus could fix that. 'First Mate, would you mind taking the wheel, please?'

'Aye aye, Cap'n,' was the reply. 'Where we headed? To battle? To discover new lands?

Is it anything in particular we're after, Cap'n?
A white whale, maybe? Aarrrrr!'

That was a new one, thought Atticus. First
Mate was funny, too. In his mind it couldn't
be more perfect.

'There's something I have to do,' he said.
'First things first, eh?'

First Mate nodded with a raised chin and
squinty eyes. Atticus took off for the captain's
quarters, certain from First Mate's expression
that he was trying to hold in a fart.

Is that a wee spout on the horizon?

Chapter 11

Captain's Quarters

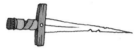

It was dark below deck, but once he pulled back the heavy curtains it was okay. A waft of something soupy was coming up from the galley. Like everyone else, Atticus had a hammock to sleep in, but he had this room to himself. There was a desk and a chair and the roll of stuff he'd brought with him. Heavy, treasury chests were against the wall. There was a wardrobe, a mirror and

Filling this soup with ink—then taking my chances with the dolphins.

that was pretty much it. He'd seen it all before, of course, but it felt new with the sound of water slapping against the hull.

Atticus unfurled his flag and stared at it. What a beauty. Tough and scary and mean and piratey.

'Harrrr aarrrrrr!' came his whispered growl. With his pirate shirt and hat on, he looked to the mirror and smiled. 'Cap'n,'

he said, 'you ready to get piratin'?' After looking around the room to make sure he really was alone, he winked. 'Aye aye,' he said back to himself.

There was only one way to start.

'A list,' he whispered.

1. Hoist flag.
2. Shoot cannons. ☺
2.5 Make someone walk the plank.

3. Find treasure ...

)SWAP

4. ▾ Find a treasure map.

POP

5. Shoot cannons again.
6. Eat.
7. Find more treasure.

8. Look for a white whale.

9. Give the white whale
   a cool name.
   Miby Dook? Dicky Mobs?
   Richard Moby? Moby Rich!

10. Have a fight with the white whale.

11. Loose a leg and get a peg.

12. Let the Moby Rich escape
    so we can find him again.

13. Tell people the story of Moby Rich.

14. Find more treasure.

15. Eat.

Something was definitely cooking. Atticus rubbed his tummy and looked around. Even though he knew the heavy chests were empty, he decided to check again, just in case. At the very least, he knew his treasure would have a home. It was simply a matter of finding some.

'Imagine if someone's snuck some in while I wasn't looking,' he hoped aloud. 'And to get it, all I have to do is pick the right chest.'

But which chest should he pick?

Chest number one, or two or three? But imagine if there was treasure in one of the chests, and the other two had dumb things in them – like especially dumb things for a pirate ship. A puppy, or gumboots, or a month's worth of oranges, or a lemon tree. Atticus got all wound up because he thought that would actually be a really cool game to play in front of lots of people. Like a show, but a game, too. A game show. Pick a chest!

'Chest number three,' he said. 'No. No. Number two. No. Number three. Number three.' Standing at chest number three, he opened it slowly, as if it really was a game or a show. *Of course there'll be nothing inside*, he thought. *But what if? What if?*

Chest No. 1   Chest No. 2   Chest No. 3

'What if' was right! He couldn't believe it. He wanted to jump up and down and hug himself. And scream something ridiculous like, 'Oh my Gooood! Oh my Goooood!'

Inside chest number three was a box,

COMPASS
Always points north!
But feel free
to travel in any
direction you choose.

Navigational
thingy
(The Sextant)
Uses mirrors,
the sun, the
horizon and
measurments
to help you
find your way.

which most
definitely had not
been there before.
He hoiked it out and put it on the
desk. It was full of ship stuff – so
maybe it had been there and he
hadn't noticed. There were charts and maps,
a really cool pull-out telescope, a sextant,
a compass, log books with room to write
in and – was that what he thought it was?

Was that a . . .?

It couldn't be. It was too simple,
much too easy. He thought he'd have
to go to some remote village in a
far-off land full of giant mosquitos
and beating drums and weird totem
poles with droopy ears and stuff like
that. An island where a man with a bone

through his nose would try to spear him alive or boil him in a huge pot of steaming oil.

Chest number three was exactly the last place he'd expected to find a treasure map.

But there it was, near the bottom. Between one of Grandnan's old shopping lists and *The Complete Book of Knots*.

A real-life treasure map. For real!

Some impossible-to-read scrawly writing, a trail of ink in a wobbly kind of path and a great big, dirty circle over where the treasure was hidden, then the trail continued. It was obviously the escape route they were going to need after going into mortal combat to get the treasure. Atticus could barely breathe from the excitement of it.

A map. Followed by a battle. Then treasure. Then escape.

Could anyone's life get any better than this?

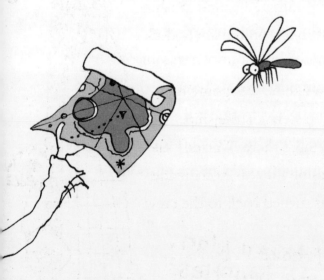

Chapter 12

The Plan

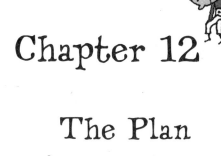

'I have a plan, me hearties,' said Atticus, practically erupting from below deck. 'A plan for *us*. Gather round.'

The crew gathered round, pushing into a tight bunch on the lower deck. Everyone except Wrong Way Warren, who looked like he was going to jump off the stern of the ship.

'While you're there, Warren,' said Atticus, tossing him his homemade flag. Atticus turned back to the crew and said,

'I have a plan, me hearties.'

Muscles was in the middle, front and centre polishing a cannonball.

There was Princess, Two Times, Stinkeye and Fishface to her left. Mullet, Buttface, Magic Harry, Slapfoot and Hogbreath to her right.

Silent Type appeared from nowhere and Lightning Rod was up the back, making sparks by sliding his knife up and down the flint.

'Give the Cap'n an *aarrr*!' barked First Mate.

'Ar?' went the crew.

'That's it? That's all yer got, yer pack of squibbers?' went First Mate. 'Aaarrrr!!!'

'Aaar!'

It was a little better.

'We're having *aarrrr* classes later – no excuses!' First Mate barked. 'Whadayagot, Cap'n? What's the plan?'

Atticus could barely contain himself. 'If we were real, dead-set pirates, what is the single most exciting thing we could do? As in, not *pretending* to be pirates in a cubbyhouse in the backyard, *acting* like we're sailing on one of the six seas –'

'Seven,' corrected Princess.

'Seven seas. Yes, of course. We're not in a cubby pretending to be pirates, with Mum or Dad throwing buckets of water on us as if it's spray from the sea.'

There was silence. And lots of frowns. He'd lost them, which was fine, because Atticus had kind of lost himself. 'Oh, come on. We've all done that, haven't we? Okay, forget that. What's the best thing we could do right now because we really are pirates?'

Buttface was first to speak. 'Join a tribe of headhunters. Get some new heads?'

'Aaaaaaah!'

went Atticus, a little exasperated.

'Aaaaarrh!'

went the crew with genuine feeling.

Let's write a comic opera about us. We can fight, wear tights, sing and sail the six seas.

seven!—

We'll call our show
The Pirates of Fate & Chance
or
The Pirates who Sing & Dance

How about...
The Pirates in Penal Pants?

'Much better,' cheered First Mate. 'Much, much better! Youse are getting it now.'

Atticus put his hands in the air and calmed everyone down. When he had their attention, he eyeballed the lot of them and said very quietly, 'Doesn't anyone want to find some . . .' and he started to spell it out. 'T·R·E·A-'

'Treacle?' said Fishface. 'You've got treacle? Yum.'

Treatment for my rash.

'Wait. Hang on, Fishface. Not finished yet. T.R.E.A.S –'

'Trees? You want to find trees?' Stinkeye looked unhappy. But that was his usual face.

Treadmill.

Atticus rolled his eyes and waved the treasure map at them. 'Who wants to go and get some treaaaaasuuurre??'

Treaties, treaties!

'Ahhaaaaarrrrrrrr!!!' went the crew. 'Treasure!' they roared. It was on, like an electric shock had gone through the ship. Lightning Rod was fully lit up.

'To the treasure!' yelled Atticus. He held the map in front of him and pointed out to sea. 'That way,' he said, before rotating the map. 'Or that way.'

Aaaaarrr!

'Such a funny Cap'n!' said First Mate, looking over his shoulder at the map. 'It's probably that way.'

'Hoist the flag, Warren! We're on the hunt for treasure,' said Atticus.

Warren did as he was told, holding the flag to the last possible second so it could unfurl itself in spectacular style. It was almost perfect.

'Wrong way, Warren.'

Chapter 13

A Treasure Hunt

If finding the treasure map had been easy, working out what it meant was a bit more complicated.

There wasn't much sense to the map. The route did circles and doubled back on itself and, 'To be honest,' said Atticus, 'looking at it now, it's as if a beetle has wandered through an ink spot and stumbled across the page. And what are these scribbles? Is it writing?'

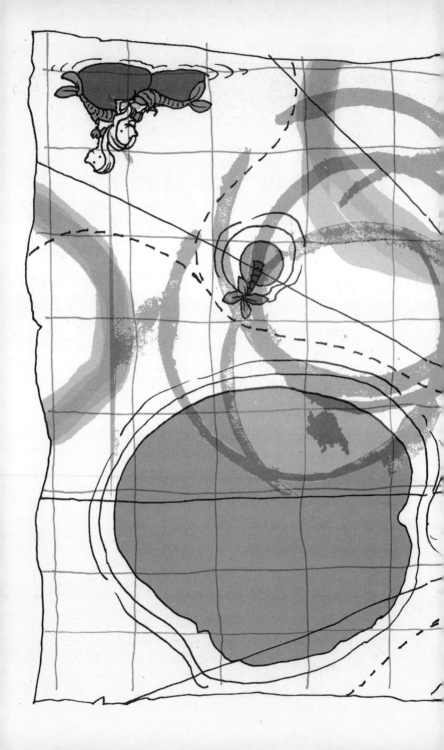

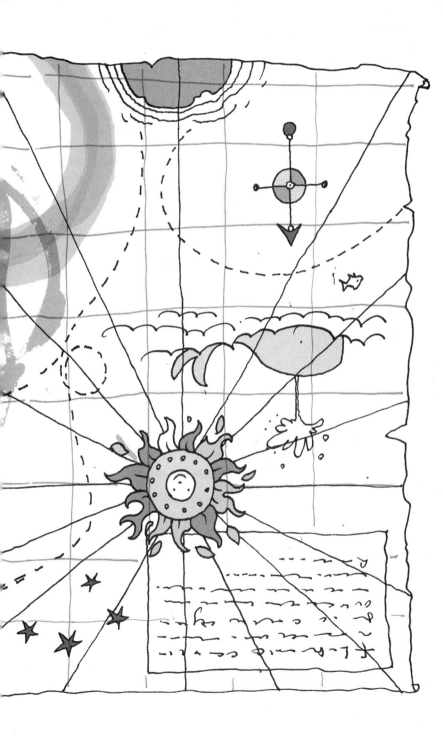

First Mate and Harry nodded. 'Hmmm,' they went together. Magic Harry spoke first. 'It might say "bacon", but then it looks like a whale. I think it's a whale. These here must be whale grounds. And this here looks like two mermaids sitting on a rock. Dang. I knew they were real. But the circle . . . why would they put a circle there?' He pointed. 'And not there. Or there? Maybe it's a trick. Maybe they're trying to confuse us, throw us off the scent, make us question what it really means.'

Harry then asked Atticus for the spyglass and looked around the ship. 'Giant Spider! We're under attack!' he squealed.

AAAAA AAARGH!

First Mate grabbed the spyglass, looked at the end and flicked the daddy-long-legs onto the deck.

We're under ATTACK!

Magic Harry tried again. 'I think I see it now, Cap'n.' He pointed from the horizon to the map. 'That land there is this land here. That land is this land. This land is that land.' He looked at the map. 'This land is your land. This land is my land,' he kind of sang.

'Oh, la-di-dah,' went First Mate.

'Whoever made this map was either a genius or dizzy from too much fizzy drink. For sure

He he he he he

that circle means something. We just have to work out what it is,' Magic Harry said,

Nice One Dad.

getting more excited. 'We go that way.'

'You sure, Harry?' asked Atticus.

Sail away
Sail away
Sail away

First Mate was already sure. 'Make sail, squibbers! Hoist away. Way haul away, haul away, would youse! We's after some treasure now!'

As each sail went up, *The Grandnan* got that little bit faster. She seemed to rise in the water as the crew rose to the challenge at hand.

'She's a beauty, ain't she?! We're surely close to flying!' Atticus was giddy.

Harry plotted a course and tweaked the direction of the ship.

She rose in the water again.

'We's flying, Captain. We's actually flying,' said Stinkeye. He was at the side of the ship, waving at Atticus but pointing to the water.

Atticus looked around. For a fairly rough sea this was an exceptionally smooth ride. He went to the side of the ship and peered over the edge. They were not in the water, but above it. They were flying. Literally. 'What magic is this, Harry?' he roared.

Magic Harry shrugged. 'It's something I've been working on. You like?'

'Permission to approach,' said Muscles.

'Of course,' went Atticus.

She made a pointing motion at the bottom of the ship. 'It's the stand. On the bottom of the ship. The keel, Cap'n. It's making the ship rise out of the water.' Atticus had no idea what she was talking about. 'The stand,' she went, again. 'I don't know what you'd call it. It's like a wing or a foil for the ship's keel. I think it's literally lifting us up, out of the water.'

She put her arms out wide, as if she was a bird flying. 'Wings, you know? *The Grandnan*'s got wings. We'll be the fastest ship on the seas,' she said. 'There's practically no drag on the hull.'

They were surely soaring now. The wind was up and blowing hair and hope all over the place. Atticus held tight to the wheel as Magic Harry kept them on course for the treasure. Not one single crew member aboard *The Grandnan* would have been anywhere else for anything.

Mullet flicked his hair and opened his lungs to a song. He was like a rock star up there at the bow of the ship, his long rat's tails blowing in the wind. Muscles was suddenly worried. *What if he falls?* She moved in behind him and hung on.

> *'We's a flyin' on the seas,*
> *Lookin' for some treasure.*

I hate the taste of peas
When you're sailing into weather.'

Everyone except Silent Type sang along.
It was joyous.

'Sailing into weather.
Sailing into weather.'

Mullet stopped singing. 'Oh crap!
We's sailing into weather.'

Chapter 14

The Perfect Storm

The wind was solid now. It had steadily increased from a decent blow to something of a gale. And the storm loomed large, taking up much of the sky in front of them. Behind, it still looked just about serene.

Then the waves came up, in a big way.

Atticus had the wheel and tried to turn it, but it was as if *The Grandnan* was on rails. They were on a collision course with nature's fury. 'She won't turn. She won't turn!' he hollered. 'Muscles! I need Muscles!'

Magic Harry was next to him, yelling. 'It's the winged keel. We're going so fast it's working like a giant rudder. We have to slow down or we're all going to diiiiieeeeeee!'

Muscles jumped up to the bridge and grabbed hold of the wheel. With all her might she pulled and she pulled, and ever so slowly *The Grandnan* began to turn away from the storm and diagonally up the face of an enormous wave.

'NOOOOOOOO!' wailed First Mate.
'If there's one thing I know about sailing,
it's that you can't go up a giant wave sideways.
You have to hit it front on. You have to
show it who's boss, that you're not scared.
It's almost impossible for a wave to roll
a ship front to back, but it'll smash you
from the side every single time!'

Muscles looked to her captain. Atticus
leapt for the wheel and helped her wrench it
back in the direction it'd just come from. *The
Grandnan* lurched and fought, but they got her
in a straight line facing up the first, giant wave.

'YEESSSS!' roared First Mate. 'That's the
way. That's iiiiiit!'

'We have to slow down – to
get control of the ship!' Magic

Complaining
pirates!
Try being me!

Harry shouted above the
wind. 'Slow her down,
Captain.'

'Mumma! Mumma?!
I want my muuuumma!' It came
from deep in the ship, where
a bunch of the crew were huddled
together, hiding from the horror.
It could have been anyone.

Things had got very bad, very quickly –
much faster than Atticus could have imagined.
His pirating dream had never included a
moment like this, where the wind blew so hard
it whipped the logic out of his brain. He had
no idea what to do. They were under attack
from the waves ahead, which were marching
forwards like an army, row after row after row.

Even at home, in the safety of his own
house, he'd been a bit of a sook in a storm,
hiding under his bed with his blankets around
him and a nightcap pulled down tight over

his head. He should have known it would be a billion times worse being tossed around the ocean in Grandnan's old ship if a storm came knocking, shouldn't he? Of course he should!

But he never considered piratin' could actually be dangerous. Now he wanted to holler for his mum as well. But there wasn't time, or even any point. She was miles away, probably chomping scones and supping tea. The violent, ugly song of a sail flapping hard against the mast made him look up. 'The sails!' he yelled above the roar of the ocean. 'We have to save the sails!'

Lightning Rod was still in the crow's nest, his face beaming. He had his hands out wide, as if summoning the energy of the storm. 'No whales,' he yelled down the mast. 'Can't see any whales. No whales to save today, Captain.'

'SAILS! SAILS! SAVE THE SAILS! SAVE THE SAILS!'

Did he say 'Show your tails'?

I think he said 'Save the snails'.

The problem was obvious to Atticus. Because the wind was so strong, the sails were pulling the ropes really, really tight. To get the sails down, they had to loosen the ropes, but they were literally too tight to loosen. Not even Muscles was strong enough to do it, and she was awesome!

The first sail ripped. It was a sickening sound. Like a baby crying when you pull its toes and try to crack the knuckles.

'Waaaaaaaaaah!'

'Cut the ropes, Cut the ropes!'

Save the Sails

yelled Two Times. He was out from behind the shelter and charging along the deck, holding a tomahawk high in the air. Once he'd cut the low ropes, he scrambled up the front mast to the boom, hacking the ropes there. As each sail flapped, Fishface, Mullet, Silent Type, Hogbreath and Muscles dragged the sails into the booms, tying them off and saving them.

It was a brilliant display of teamwork, and *The Grandnan* was losing speed.

From the foremast to the aft, they worked, only losing a couple of the lighter, smaller sails. Atticus yelled out for them to leave two sails, half sheeted, on the aft-mast for stability.

Against the odds, his plan seemed to work.

It didn't make the storm go away, which was unleashing a very wet and horrible hell upon one and all. But they did get control of *The Grandnan*. She dropped back off the keel and kind of settled into the water, which

hack
hack

part 3

Stowaway Puppy

It had been a long time between meals.

Seeing something delicious to chew, he climbed high above the pirate crew...

and leapt for his dinner...

grabbing what he thought was a bowl of bones.

Splash

To be continued...

seemed to steady her and everyone on board. The waves still battered them, and the wind still whistled through the ropes.

It rained or it poured and the noise of it was awful. But they fought on. Fighting up the front of swells, racing down the back of them. It was rough. They were scared. The odd cries for 'mumma' continued.

In the crow's nest, Lightning Rod was loving it. When everyone else ducked for cover from the crack of lightning or bark

of thunder, he launched a fist in the air and
*Aarrrrrr*ed!

The Grandnan held fast. She rose and she
fell at the whim of the storm and yet she
fought on. What a ship she was!

And then, almost as suddenly as it had
begun, it was over.

It was as if they'd sailed into a violent,
treacherous beast of a storm, attacked and
slashed, then survived to the other side.
There were cries of 'Yes!' and 'Ripper!' and
'You little beauty!' The cries for Mumma were
no more.

'We survived,' wailed Princess, as if she
hadn't expected to. 'We survived!'

On the verge of dancing
a merry jig, everyone rejoiced.
And then they heard an excited
voice from above. 'I don't think it's
over just yet! Eyes skyward, would youse!'

As one, the crew looked up to the crow's
nest. It was Lightning Rod, smouldering like
a forgotten fire. 'Has anyone heard of the eye
of the storm?' he said, almost in a whisper,
as if he was trying not to wake a baby or your
little brother when you want to sneak out of
the house without him knowing so you can
get hold of his bike and take the seat off and
watch his eyes pop out when he jumps on it
to go for a ride.

Lightning Rod pointed straight up. Directly
above them was a circle. 'Does that look like
an eye to anyone else?'

Stinkeye nodded. 'Now *that* is an eye!'

The air was suddenly so still. Compared
to the mishmash they'd just been in, it was

utterly surreal. Then, very
very gently, the air began to
move around them. Not a
normal kind of wind, but a
circle kind of wind. Around
and around. Then the sea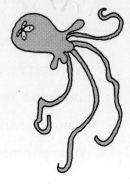
got hold of what was going
on and must have dug it, because the ocean
started doing circles as well. Not to be
left out, *The Grandnan* got into the spin
of things, too.

 Around. And
around. And around.

'What's going ooooon?'

'WHAT'S HAAAAAAPPENiiiiing?'

Spinning. Frothing. Turning. Around and
around.

Princess held tight to the rail with one
hand and cuddled the baby with the other.
She went completely white and screamed.

AAAAA AAAR

The Grandnan, with all who sailed on her, spun faster and faster as the water around her rose into a mighty, spinning column of water. As Princess tried to find her feet, her heels clicked together. She wailed, 'I want to go home. I want to go home!' But it was no use. No one was going anywhere except up and around and around.

They were in the middle of a water spout and there was literally not a thing they could do about it. 'Hang on! Everyone, hang on!' Atticus yelled to his crew. 'We've seen worse than this. We are Van Tasticus. We can survive anything!'

A fish was spat out of the water spout, landing with a slap on the deck. Then another. And another. Soon it was raining fish.

Then a jellyblubber hit the deck. And a squid and prawns and even one or two scallops.

'Mamamia!' yelled Atticus, ducking for cover. But for all the world it sounded like 'marinara'.

And there was more rain and thunder and lightning while the ship spun like a top and Lightning Rod screamed, 'Is that all you got?!'

That's when a massive shark went WHUMP! on the deck.

It was too much for Atticus.

His brain couldn't process another thing.

Chapter 15

Was It a Dream?

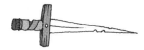

It was the sun coming
through the window
that woke Atticus.

Before opening his eyes,
he reached for the magic talking
glass the funny looking one-eyed green stick
men had given him. *Whoa! What a dream.*
It had started so normal with the whole
Grandnan thing. But then it got weird with
the pirate thing, Hulk and Hogan and the
winged keel and smouldering Lightning Rod
and big, tall Muscles. *Wow!* Atticus tried to
remember what he'd had for dinner. Maybe
there was too much chilli in his con carne.
It always made his dreams awesome.

Atticus's dream
(the bit that he Missed)
Return to pod return to pod.
Where will we holiday now?
Beam me up, girls.
Beep beep
Clink clink
snip snip
Snap Snap
ZZZZZZZZZ

But once he opened his eyes, Atticus saw he was in his hammock, back in the captain's quarters.

When he stuck his head out the door to the deck, he saw Mullet and Hogbreath pushing fish into a pile. Fishface looked like he'd found a pretty one and was giving it a kiss. Atticus wasn't dreaming.

Best of all, he was alive.

The Grandnan was in good shape, too. Pretty much. Both masts standing, the booms fastened. There were ripped sails up the top and a lot of dangling ropes, but all in all, she looked pretty good. The crew was all there, cleaning or polishing or doing jobs. And he smelt food. Fish, he figured, given they now had enough on deck to keep them stuffed for a week at least.

'Cap'n Atticus is awake, First Mate,' came the call from above. It was Stinkeye. He had the spyglass stuck into the loop of his belt. 'He looks okay, sir.'

Atticus gave Stinkeye a wink and a relaxed salute. 'At ease,' he said. 'Alas, I am most definitely okay. Though I'm not really sure what happened.'

First Mate went to Atticus and stood before him, hands behind his back. At ease. 'Well, Cap'n,' came the whisper, 'it seems you fell asleep.'

'Fell asleep? How?' It seemed impossible to Atticus that could happen. 'The last thing I remember, we were being sucked up the middle of an enormous water spout. There were fish and squid and jellyblubbers flying all over the place. And a shark. I remember an

enormous shark.' He looked around the ship
as if it might come out of hiding to get him.

'All true,' said First Mate. 'All so very true.'

'And the shark? Where it be?'

'In the drink, where she should be,' said
Fishface. 'Here, off the back of our ship.
She's a beauty, ain't she? Real friendly, too.'
Atticus peered over the stern without getting
too close. Sure enough, off the back of *The
Grandnan* came a huge, toothy grin. Fishface
was tossing fish scraps to the mum of Jaws.
'You never know when a lady like this might
come in handy.' He smiled, sending another
morsel off the back of the boat.

'Don't feed it, Fishface!' said Atticus.
'It'll never leave. What if we want to have
a swim? Jump off the plank? Catch a fish?
Have a wash? It'll eat us, won't it?'

'Not this one.' Fishface winked again. 'We's friends, we are. She's a good little sharky. Ain't ya?' The shark went back under water. 'No worries about this one, matey. You'll see.'

Atticus shrugged. It seemed ridiculous, but Fishface might be right. Maybe sharks could be friendly. He made a note to have more of an open mind while looking at the trail of foam behind his ship.

That's when the shark came out of the water. Not just the head, or the tail, or

the huge fin, but the whole dang lot of it. Straight out and up and towards the back of the ship. Right in line with Fishface. The eyes had rolled back in its head and its massive toothy gob was going GNAR! GNAR! GNAR! as it opened and closed. If that wasn't an attack, Atticus had no idea what was. The massive fish slammed into the back of the ship with a huge crack, before sliding down the stern and into the water.

'Cute, ain't she? Comin' up for a kiss like that?' Fishface was gushing.

'Do NOT feed that SHARK again,'

roared First Mate. Fishface nodded, kicking one final scrap into the ocean. There was a slurp from behind the boat.

'So, there was a shark,' said Atticus. 'Part of me hoped that might have been a dream.

How long was I asleep for? And how did
I just fall asleep?'

Princess, who'd been listening, came up
with a cup of something hot for Atticus.
'You just . . . fell asleep. Like, you were
standing up and then your eyes went all
googly and rolled back in your head. After
that, you were lying down. I remember
thinking, I wish I could fall asleep that fast.'

First Mate leaned in and whispered,
'You might have fainted, Cap'n.'

'Oh, no. Not me. I always fall asleep like
that.' Atticus nodded to Princess. 'Always.
And how long did I sleep for? Did I miss
much?'

Everyone shook their heads. While

Sing you a lullaby!

A Sea Shanty perhaps

pretending to do other things, the crew had
been listening in.

'Nothing? I didn't miss anything at all?'

'Well,' said Hogbreath, 'there was the –'

'There was nothing. Nothing at all,'
everyone else said through clenched teeth.

'Good then, sometimes I get
a bit worried about missing out.
Not a fear, as such. Not a Fear
Of Missing Out. Laugh Out
Loud, right?'

Silent Type gave him the look.
He knew exactly what his captain
was talking about. LOL.

Chapter 16

A New Plan

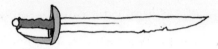

'Cap'n Atticus, sir. Your orders? The plan?'
First Mate rocked from foot to foot.

Atticus pushed back his hat and
straightened his shirt. He'd been thinking
about everything *but* a plan to this point. The
ship looked fine, the ropes had been retied,
he'd missed pretty much nothing when he'd
nodded off. He patted his pants, then his
shirt, as if looking for something. 'The map.
Where's the map? Let's go get that treasure.'

'Treasure!'

fist-pumped First Mate.

°○○○○ Awkward! ○○

Time to invent
a secret handshake.

Treasuuuuuuuuureaaagh!

The crew started a chant, and Silent Type got jiggy with a brand-new hand dance. 'Trea-sure. Trea-sure. Trea-sure.'

Atticus kept time but changed the words. 'Where's the map? Where's the map? Where's the map?'

'Where's the map?' said First Mate. 'Do you mean the treasure map?'

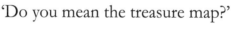

He don't say much but dang he can shake it.

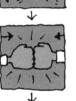

It was one of those weird moments where everyone looked at everyone else to see if they knew where the map was. For Atticus, it reminded him of going fishing with his dad. And his dad would say, 'Who's got the bait?' Atticus and his brother knew one of them would have been asked to get the bait before they left home, and both of them would always forget. Instead of saying,

'We forgot it' or something smart, they'd just look at each other and pat their pockets, as if the bait might somehow be hiding there.

When First Mate said 'Where's the map?', it gave Atticus that old feeling. He patted his pockets again before saying, 'I don't think I was last to touch the treasure map. Was it you?'

First mate patted his pockets and shook his head. 'Magic Harry?'

'Nope.'

'Are you sure, Magic Harry? Remember? Didn't you have it last?'

Magic Harry winced. 'Maybe not last. I showed it to, um, Princess. Who definitely touched it . . .' he said as he looked around to see everyone not looking at him, '. . . and then I, um, I, ah, put it in the, um . . .' Then he looked to the ship's wheel. 'There. I put it in the gap between the wheel and the wheel-holder thing.'

Sure enough, there was a piece of paper wedged in there. Mullet was closest. He reached for the paper and gave it a tug, but the corner pulled away in his fingers.

'Aarrrrr! Careful, you squibber!'

barked First Mate. 'It'll still be damp from the storm, you dingbat. Gently, gently.'

Muscles went to the helm, making First Mate roll his eyes. He guessed the map was doomed for sure. But instead of tugging on the paper, she pulled on the wheel, making the gap in the wood larger, Mullet was then able to get at the map without using any force at all.

'Clever Muscles,' clapped First Mate.

The others joined in. 'Clever Muscles.

Clever Muscles. Clever Muscles.' But it didn't really catch on.

Mullet handed the map to Atticus, who unfolded the page. How could he have been so stupid? To leave the map out in the elements was a silly, beginner's mistake. His only hope was that the treasure map would be all right.

Which, of course . . .

. . . it wasn't.

'**Curses,**' slumped Atticus. 'What'll we do, now?' He let the map fall to the deck and leaned against the mast. No one spoke, which was good, because he wasn't really asking for an answer. Or maybe he was, but when none came, he looked up to the sky. It was so blue, such a rich, beautiful colour, one he'd never seen before.

So light and bright.

He had a sudden urge to be in it. Atticus climbed the rope ladder up the main mast, slowly to begin with. Once past the first boom, he was on the shimmy. Up and up and up, until he could climb no more. Instead of hopping into the crow's nest, he scrambled to the end of the boom.

'Careful, Cap'n,' came the call from below.

But Atticus was fine. He couldn't believe he hadn't been up here before. It was so fantastic to be up high and free and piratin'. Something had definitely changed. It wasn't just the sky and the smell in the air; it was everything. Even the water looked different. It was clearer, as if he could see all the way into the heart of the ocean.

He'd really done it, he'd left his home behind,

and after battling through the storm from
hell, he'd arrived in a whole new world. With a
start, Atticus realised that even if he wanted to,
turning *The Grandnan* for home wasn't a realistic
option. He'd come too far for that.

For the first time in ages, he thought of his
mum and dad.

What would they be thinking? Were they
sad? Did they miss him? His mum would be

the first to tell him to be careful standing up there on the highest boom; it had to be the most dangerous point of the ship. His dad would probably tell him to jump off for fun. Atticus wondered if they'd be proud of him for coming this far. For becoming a captain and having a crew that seemed to like him. *Look at them down there*, he thought, *working hard on* The Grandnan, *swabbing the decks, coiling the ropes. What a crew. What a crew!*

For sure his mum and dad'd be impressed.

Atticus smiled to himself. Grandnan would be wrapped that he'd made such a good choice, too. This was the whole point, right? To choose something with your heart, not your head. To make something good of yourself, and to be happy. He had a clear

picture of his mum and dad. If they could
see him now, they would definitely think he'd
made a great choice.

Definitely.

Atticus looked back to the heavens and
closed his eyes.

Brrrrrrp!

Splaaaat!

'Eeeww!'

went Atticus. He wiped the bird poop out
of his eye. Above him, the most colourful
bird he'd ever seen squawked as it wheeled in
the sky. 'That's new, too,' he said to himself.
'I haven't seen a bird for a long time. Wait a
minute. If there's a bird, there must be –'

Chapter 17

Land Ho!

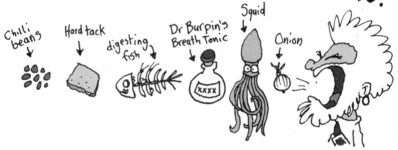

It was Hogbreath in the crow's nest. Atticus could smell his yell almost before he heard it. It was worse than a fur seal on a hot day.

'Westward. Or eastward. There. That-a-way.'

That wasn't me

Atticus stood tall on the boom and
scanned the horizon. Sure enough, far, far
to the east there was something sticking out
of the water. It could be land, but without a
decent spyglass it was hard to tell.

Hogbreath was looking through the smaller
spyglass, but Atticus knew he had a bigger one
in his cabin.

'First Mate,' he sang out, 'get me the big
spyglass, would yer? I'm coming down!' With
that, Atticus edged to end of the boom, tried
not to think too much and launched into
the water.

What Atticus saw was most definitely land,
just not much of it. And maybe, just maybe,
there was something else. He ever so gently
twisted the eyepiece on his spyglass to change
the focus.

Princess cleared her throat and said,
'Captain?'

Atticus said, 'What?'

'Captain?'

He said, 'What?'

'I said, Caaaaaaaaaptain?'

'I said, what? What you want?' said Atticus, with a bit of a snap. He was concentrating very hard, trying to work out what else was on the little island.

'Uh, Captain Atticus? You might want to see this.'

Atticus turned to Princess, who was pointing to the west.

'Out there, on the other horizon?' she asked. 'Is that a ship, Captain?'

They'll never fall for it again. It's too soon, Dad. Too soon!

Whatch this.

All eye's on me.

GiANT SPiDER

Every time! Ha ha ha

'Aarrrrr! Shiver me timbers,' barked First Mate. 'What are the chances? We see nothing for ages and then we see land and a ship in the same day? Sheesh.'

With a bit of tuning, Atticus was just able to bring the ship into focus.

It was a loooong way off. 'It's definitely a ship,' he said. 'A galleon, by the looks of it.'

'Aaarrrrr,' went First Mate. 'There's a ship, me hearties.'

'There's people on it, a bit like ours!'

'Aaarrrrr, what kind of people?' First Mate sidled up to Atticus, desperate for a look through the spyglass. 'Are they trading type people? Or treasure type people? Do they have beards with jewels in 'em? Big golden, hoopy earrings? Studs in their noses? How many cannons? It doesn't matter, really. We're fast enough to dodge cannons, anyway.'

'There's cannons, all right. And big, golden hoopy earrings . . . and . . . and . . .'

The strangest feeling came over Atticus, like he was standing in front of a heater on a very hot day. He felt a flush go through him, or a wave of warmth at the very least. He tightened the focus again to confirm that the captain on the other ship was like no captain he'd ever imagined.

'Did you say jewellery?' barked First Mate. 'Turn *The Grandan* about. You've said enough, Cap'n Atticus. The island will always be there, but treasure's got a habit of disappearin'. Prepare to attack. Prepare to attaaaaaaaack! Give me an *aaaaarrrrrr*!'

'Aaaaarrr!'

warbled the crew. They were getting much better at their *aarrrrrs*, though there was still a way to go.

'Cap'n, if I may be so bold.' First Mate was almost bowing to Atticus. He had one hand behind his back, the other rolling in the air in front of him. 'As this is our first time in the thick of it, can I suggest you put on your best captain's kit? Something special, something to remember the moment by? We've got time, for shizzle. And if you like, I'll get Buttface to get his paints out. We should capture this, sir. The making of our very first enemy, the taking of our very first treasure. Aaarrrrrr! As we prepare to battle, sir, prepare for history.'

Atticus was genuinely moved. He actually did have a special pirate outfit that he was dead keen to try out, but so far, there hadn't been the occasion.

He passed First Mate the spyglass and said, 'Take the wheel, my friend. And if

Buttface could get his paints, that would be grand. You're right. We should remember this forever.'

With that, Atticus headed below, more nervous than anything else. His first pirate fight. Wow!

'Oh Captain, my Captain,' said First Mate affectionately. Then to the crew,

'Get ready, squibbers!'

he roared.

'Cannons, powder, flints !!!

We's only as good as our last fight, so let's not make it this one!'

It took Mullet and Buttface a moment to figure out what that meant. First Mate put the spyglass to his eye and fiddled with the focus.

'Huh?' he said, before putting the spyglass down and rubbing his eye. 'Could it be?'

He gave both ends a clean and looked again.

Chapter 18

Another Plan

Below deck, Atticus was pumped.

'Better get this right,' he said, scratching round for a piece of paper and a quill. While getting dressed, he scribbled a list.

1. Find cannon balls.
2. Load cannons. ← SWAP
3. Find gunpowder. ↩
4. Get rope swings ready.
5. Grappling hooks.
6. Swords.
7. Boarding planks.
~~Swords~~
8. TREASURE CHEST!!

Atticus stood before the mirror in his finest livery.

Exciting didn't cover it. Even though he'd never say it aloud, Atticus was wrapped by what he saw. Pants to just above the ankles, jacket near the knees, and the epaulets on the shoulders made the whole outfit zing. Atticus got his belt and sword in order, and thought Buttface could make a pretty good go of how he looked. Swinging the eye patch on his finger, he knew it was over the top. And whilst the hook he'd found did look pretty funky sticking out the end of his shirt, he worried he'd poke his eye out if he got an itch. Then he really would need the eye patch.

Atticus was as ready as he'd ever be. Coming up from down below, he stepped on deck with a hearty, 'Aarrrrrrrrrr, ye ready, me hearties? Is it time to chaaaaarge?'

He held his sword high in the air, fully expecting to see the other ship within

Aaaaarrrr! Ye ready, me Hearties?

The lighting is perfect.

attacking distance and Buttface sketching the moment.

But there was nothing. He looked the other way. More nothing. Off the bow of the boat he saw something. Possibly a teeny-weeny island with what looked like one skinny palm tree, but that was about it.

'Where's the ship? Where'd it go?' whispered Atticus to First Mate, looking around as if he was about to be tackled. 'I thought we was goin' piratin'!'

First Mate walked quickly to his captain, hands out like he was weighing two invisible sacks of gold. 'Ermmm, it's the strangest thing, Captain. She took off. She must have seen us at the same time we saw her, and she hoofed it in the other direction.'

'But we chased her, didn't we?' Atticus kept an eye on the horizon, hoping to see a fresh glimpse. He was keen to find that ship, get some treasure and meet the other captain. There was something about her that made him want to know more.

'Well –'

'The other ship's definitely gone!' It was Wrong Way Warren, looking back to where they'd sailed from. 'Definitely disappeared now.'

Atticus looked up to Warren. He couldn't quite figure out why he was looking backwards, not forwards. That's where the other ship should probably be if they were chasing it. 'Aren't you looking the wrong way, Warren?' he yelled up to the crow's nest.

'Not this time, Captain. For sure I'm not. The other ship is that way and we's going this way. Land ahoy! Land ahoy!' Wrong Way Warren was pointing off the bow of *The Grandnan*. It was most definitely the island ahead, though not much of one.

'Would you mind, Captain?' It was Buttface. He'd set up an easel and paints, and motioned for Atticus to come to the front of the ship. 'For your portrait, Captain.'

Atticus wasn't so sure. In his mind, the moment had gone. That ship had sailed, as the saying goes. All he really wanted to do was head below deck and crawl back into his normal piratin' clothes.

'Let's wait until we're ready to take our first ship, shall we?' He was totally bummed.

First Mate looped a friendly arm through

Atticus's and dragged him towards Buttface. 'Or we could get a portrait of the first time you discover a new land. Maybe name it after yourself –'

Sit straight think STRONG and loose the eye patch.

'That island's got an islander! There's someone there, on the island. And he's got a bird, Captain. And treasure, Captain. It looks like he's got treasure!!!' Wrong Way Warren was practically jumping out of the crow's nest.

'– and find your first treasure, Cap'n. What a time for a portrait!' said First Mate.

Atticus grinned. First Mate had him at 'discover a new land'. He looked through the spyglass towards the island and saw it, just as Warren had described. Smack bang in the middle of a small island was a man sitting on what looked exactly like a treasure chest.

There was something about him that was odd. Atticus fiddled with the focus, hoping to make it clearer. What kind of hat was that? Was he sunburnt? But Atticus was interrupted before the penny dropped.

Magic Harry waved the treasure map. 'You were right to turn around and stop following that ship, First Mate.' He was beaming. 'If we'd have chased it, we would have lost the trail of the treasure.'

'Huh?' Atticus foisted the spyglass back into his belt and looked from Magic Harry to First Mate. 'Weren't we chasing –'

But Harry was so excited he couldn't let him finish. 'I think I've figured the treasure map out, Captain. You see, we thought the circles were to throw us off the scent of the treasure. When, actually, the map was exactly right, sir. We had to go through the storm and get tossed and rolled and seemingly lose our way. As if we'd been through a portal. See? We followed it almost exactly. The circles we did are here, and that's where we

hit the storm. So we were on the right track
the whole time. This is us here. See? And
the island is there, right in the middle of the
circle. We did it, Captain. You did it.'

'We did, didn't we? And you knew all
along, Harry? That's just magic, that is.'

Buttface waved his brushes. 'Captain?'

'Why not?' said Atticus, letting Buttface
put him in position. 'But quickly. I want to be
ready to take the island, and if that's treasure,
we'll take that too.' He put a foot up on the
bulkhead and looked captainly.

'Excellent, Captain. Work it. Work it. That's really excellent. Dare I say it, sir, but you look so hot right now.'

Chapter 19

Idiot Island

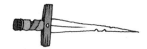

The closer they got to the island, the weirder things started to look.

The man in the hat had obviously seen *The Grandnan* – how could he not? And now it looked like he was furiously digging a hole to hide in.

'He's up to something, Captain,' went Warren from the crow's nest. 'He's digging a hole. Digging. Digging. Now he's dragging the treasure chest. Dragging . . .'

Atticus was watching through his own spyglass, but enjoying the commentary from above.

'. . . dragging. And it's in. The chest is in the hole, mostly. Now he's covering it with sand.'

There's no other
contenders
within reach...
but wait?

Atticus could see the hole he'd dug wasn't quite deep enough, so the top of the chest was still sticking out. The man covered it in sand, then a palm frond from the single palm tree. There was still something weird about him that Atticus couldn't figure out. But he would, eventually, he was sure.

Atticus lowered the spyglass, cleaned it and looked again. 'I'm not sure we'll need to go into full battle-station mode. Maybe half battle stations. It looks as if he's alone. Does anyone want to fire a warning shot to let him know we're serious?'

Lightning Rod and Mullet had heard enough. They were desperate to fire anything, so as soon as they heard the words 'warning shot' they sparked the flint and lit the fuses of every cannon on the island side of *The Grandnan*.

'Fire in the hooooooooles,'

they yelled together.

'Fire in the hooooooooles!'

Kaboom! 'oom! 'oom! 'oom!

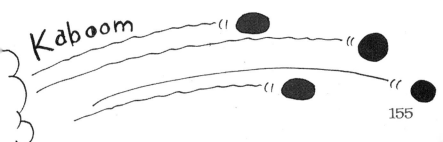

The sheer force of the four cannons blowing off together was enough to practically tip the ship. *The Grandnan* rocked to the side, then righted itself as four perfect smoke rings blew towards the island.

'**Aaaaaaaarrr!**' went the pirates.
It was their best yet.

The man on the island scurried to the back side of his palm tree. Atticus could see he was yelling, but not hear what he was saying. Whatever it was, he was turning purple with the force of it. 'Aaarrrrrr! He's hiding,' said Atticus to the crew.
'He's definitely scared. And his hat's just fallen off!'

Ooops!

The bird was off his
shoulder and heading for the boat,
squawking the whole way. When it got above
The Grandnan, it did a few circles, took aim
and fired. This time the poop missed
Atticus, landing with a splat on the deck.

'He says, *Go Away. Go Away*,' the parrot
squawked, doing a couple more big circles
above the ship and dropping another bomb.
'He says, *You'll be sorry. You'll be sorry!*' Then
it flew back towards
the island.

Princess, with her
hands on her hips,
said, 'Did that bird
just say we'll be sorry?'

'I think so,' said Atticus. He raised
his spyglass for another look to the
island. The man was gone. The island
empty. There was just the palm tree
and the mound where he'd hidden

the treasure. *But how?* thought Atticus. 'Where did you go?' he whispered to himself. 'What magic is this? How did you just disappear?'

First Mate asked for the spyglass. 'He is. He's gone.'

'He's gooooone!' yelled Wrong Way Warren from above. 'Island Man has vanished.'

It was Magic Harry's turn to ask for the spyglass. 'Wow. He really is gone. Maybe there's a secret stairway. Or he's invented a way to disappear. This will sound ridiculous – like truly mad – but what if he has some kind of cloak that makes him invisible? Like a shroud he covers himself with so he can't be seen? Or the tiny island isn't really a tiny island, but a huge underground fortress, and there's cannons and guns and escape hatches. What if there's an army hidden away in secret holes, and they're waiting for us to get close enough and then blow us to smithereens? What if the guy in the stupid golden hat is just a decoy? What if it's a traaaap? What if we're all about to diiiiiie?'

Harry had fully wound himself up, so much so that Muscles came along and gave him a gentle slap across the face to bring him to his senses. Well, Muscles *thought* it was gentle.

When Harry got up he said,

'Thanks, Muscles.

I needed that.'

Atticus had the spyglass again and watched on. The parrot did a couple of circles above the island, before flying behind the palm tree. It disappeared, too.

Could Harry have been right?

The parrot came out again for a quick flutter, before flying behind the palm again. Now there was nothing.

After a few seconds, the parrot was out in the open, only this time with a hand motioning for it to come back behind the tree. 'I see an arm,' said Atticus. 'And a shoulder. The parrot is now on the shoulder.' The man stuck his head out. 'There's the head, and he's back wearing his ugly fluffy hat. No panic, Harry, he's just hiding behind the palm tree.'

'Lower the jolly boats! It's time to get the treasure!' First Mate was very excited. They all were. Atticus could barely believe the way things had worked out. He thought the storm would do them in, but not only had they survived, they'd found land and treasure.

'You'll be sorry! You'll be sorry!' The parrot was back, circling, screeching, trying to nail them with poop bombs. The man on the island kept sneaking looks from behind the palm tree. Atticus figured he wasn't very smart. And his hat kept falling off, so he had to pick it up and put it back on.

'*You'll* be sorry,' said Fishface, before firing

You'll be sorry.

You'll be sorry.

no need for that.

He he he he he

161

a rock from his slingshot at the bird. He
missed by miles.

In the jolly boat on the way to shore,
Atticus turned to First Mate and asked very
quietly, 'Why did we turn around instead of
chasing that ship?'

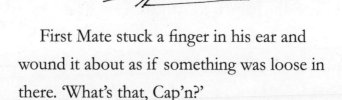

First Mate stuck a finger in his ear and
wound it about as if something was loose in
there. 'What's that, Cap'n?'

'The ship we saw? To the west. Why didn't
we chase it?'

First Mate looked about a bit before scooting up close to Atticus. In the tiniest whisper he said, 'You don't want to chase that ship, Cap'n. Any ship but that ship.'

Now Atticus looked around. 'What's wrong with that ship?'

'It's a bad ship, Cap'n. Believe me. I've heard about that ship, and that is the worst of the worst of them.'

Chapter 20

The First Attack

'Prepare to laaaaaaand!'

Two Times yelled.

Lucky they weren't hoping for a surprise attack. Atticus looked about for the other jolly boat, which was heading in another direction. He made a note to himself not to have Warren at the oars again.

They waited. Once everyone was ready, the crew of *The Grandnan* headed for the palm tree, swords and knives out, ready for battle.

'We know you're there,' said Atticus.

'There's no one here,' came the reply. 'Just me, a poor lonely parrot.'

'Doesn't sound like the parrot,' said Princess. 'Sounds like someone pretending to be a parrot.'

The parrot flew out from behind the tree and settled in the fronds at the top of the palm.

'No, just me. A simple dumb parrot,' came the voice again.

Everyone looked up to the parrot, who appeared to shake its head.

'Oh, okay,' said Atticus. 'Well, if it's just a dumb parrot, we'll go. Sorry to bother you, stupid parrot. Let's go, everyone.'

Only Warren turned to go.

'Bye,' came the voice.

'Yeah, bye,' said the entire crew of *The Grandnan*.

'Bye bye,' went Two Times.

But nobody moved.

Sure enough, the man in the mad hat looked out from behind the palm tree, to see everyone staring at him. 'Oh. You're still here.'

'Well, duh!' First Mate huffed. 'You can come out now. We don't want you. Only your treasure.'

The man shook his head, and his hat fell off. Only it wasn't his hat, it was his *hair*. *Weird*, thought Atticus. And the colour of his sunburn was more orange than red.

'Can't come out,' he said. 'And there's no treasure.'

A banana?

At least it's green!

Atticus nodded to Muscles and Mullet. 'Bring him out.'

There was a tussle. Lots of oohs and ahhs and grunts and doofs until, finally, they got him out into the open.

Atticus tried not to laugh. 'Why are you in your underpants? Where are your clothes? Who are you?'

The man straightened as much as he could without uncovering his privates. 'I am Captain Trumptee. THE Captain Trumptee! The much-feared and very scary Captain Trumptee, that's who I am. Who are you?'

Atticus stood with his feet apart, pulled his shoulders back and tilted his hat to a really cool angle. 'I am Atticus Van Tasticus. Captain of *The Grandnan*!'

The crew clapped, it sounded so good.

'And now, I'll have your treasure.' Atticus held his ground and put out his hand.

Trumptee took a step back. 'I have no treasure.'

'You do.'

'Don't.'

'Do, too.'

'Do not.'

'Aha!' said Atticus. 'So you *don't* have any treasure!'

Trumptee put a hand on his hip. 'Yes, I do.'

'Aha,' went Atticus again. 'I knew it. He has treasure!'

'Curses. You fooled me.

You are fantastic, Van Tasticus. But I'll never tell you where it is.'

Atticus walked over to the mound of sand and removed the palm frond. He then brushed away the sand, revealing the top of the treasure chest. 'Is *this* not your treasure chest?' he said.

Captain Trumptee bellowed, 'That's not a treasure chest. That's a fake treasure chest. I've never seen that chest full of treasure in my life.'

Atticus rubbed his chin. 'So, this is not the treasure chest we all just watched you bury as we approached in our pirate ship?'

'Um, no. Or hang on. Maybe. Um, yes. You might be right. I remember now. But you don't want this treasure,' Captain Trumptee said, waving one hand in front of him.

'Oh really?' Atticus looked at his crew and nodded. 'And which treasure do we want?'

It was as if they could see Captain

Trumptee relax. He even stopped covering his privates so he could point out to sea. It was gross. 'You want the other treasure. The treasure them other pirates took, the ones who came before you in the other ship.'

'The other ship?' said Atticus to First Mate. 'It must be them.' He turned to Captain Trumptee. 'When were they here?'

'Just now, pretty much,' he said. 'But you want to stay away from them. They're awful. So ugly they'd make you want to poke your own eyes out. The sight of 'em'll dry the spit out of your mouth, have you trembling in your Y-fronts. They're the freeze-your-blood-in-your-veins kind of terrible. So bad you'll be choking on your heart as it tries to run away from your body by escapin' out yer gob. Lookin' at them was like bein' awake in a nightmare!'

First Mate was quick to agree. 'I told you, Cap'n.'

'He knows it too, does he? You don't want nothin' to do with her, Mate. She's a viper!'

Atticus practically choked. 'She? This pirate monster's a *she*?'

'Aye, Captain,' nodded Trumptee. 'She's wicked. She's got half me treasure and she's got half an idea where the rest of it is hidden. Bah! I've opened me big mouth again. Curses!'

'So there's more treasure?'

'Aye,' Trumptee volunteered. 'I cannot lie.'

'He's lyin',' said Stinkeye.

The rest of the crew nodded their heads.

Trumptee looked wounded, like a four-year-old who'd just licked the top off his ice cream and watched it go splat in dog plop. 'I swear it's true. If you let me keep this treasure, I'll tell you where the rest of it is.'

Atticus looked to his crew. They were shaking their heads as if Trumptee was a kook.

Muscles piped up. 'Captain Atticus, why don't we take this treasure *and* the Captain? He can lead us to the other treasure and

part 4

Stowaway Puppy

The sea was wild... but dog paddle came naturally. splash-7-splash

The warm currents carried him to an island with only one inhabitant.

Stowaway puppy quickly buried the flag so that the strange humming man wouldn't eat it.

Run-Tum-Tugger

After living on sand & coconut juice, Stowaway Puppy almost lost hope... then two ships appeared, within hours of each other.

To be continued...

maybe even help us attack
the other pirate ship. What
do you think?'

Atticus thought the idea of
spending any time at all with
Captain Trumptee would be
pretty bruising, but Muscles
was right. 'We'll need to find
him some clothes first. The
last thing I want is to have
Captain Underpants running
around our ship.'

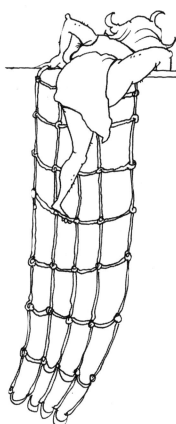

The crew had a giggle at
that. 'Captain Underpants, that
was a good one.'

Trumptee promised to open his treasure
chest once on board *The Grandnan*. He huffed
and puffed his way up the rope ladder without
help, because no one was game to touch his

undies. Muscles was surprised how heavy his chest wasn't. 'What's in this thing?' she said, rattling the chest. There was a bit of a clang and a clank, but not much. 'It's light as air.'

Once on deck, the crew circled. Everyone tried to guess what was in it. Was it jewels or gold? Was it coins or cash? Maybe something exotic they'd never heard of.

'Open it, Trumptee,' said Atticus.

The crew pressed in tighter.

Trumptee *aaarrrrr*ed. 'Me clothes. A man's got no dignity with no clothes. Let me borrow a shirt at least, then I'll open me chest, aye?'

There were mutterings among the crew, as if no one wanted to share their clothes. But it wasn't that. No one had anything that would fit. Not even Muscles. She was big, but not that big.

'There must be something,' wailed Trumptee, standing up and spreading his arms out wide. His singlet rode halfway up his guts.

'*Eeeeeeew*,' went the crew.

Muscles headed below and came back with a bundle. 'It's me biggest shirt.' But Trumptee barely got it over his head. 'Or, there's this. It's an even bigger shirt.'

Big head +
Big hair +
Big brain =
—————
BIG IDEAS

Ooo

I'm having one now!

Missed it!

No!

Trumptee put it on without even looking at it. 'Perfect,' he said. 'Now, to the treasure. Cover your eyes, or you'll be blinded by the sparkle.' He took the key from the chain at his neck and rattled it around the lock. The chest creaked open and there was indeed a sparkle.

There it goes...

Flat Top with wave & over-ear flick

The Perfect Wave

But not the kind they'd expected.

Atticus reached in, but his hand was batted away by Trumptee.

'Careful. Careful. They's very precious.' As he reached in, his hair fell off again. Trumptee set it aside and very carefully lifted something from the chest, studied it for a second, then placed it on his head.

His 'treasure' was hair. Actual goldenish coloured wigs.

'This is not treasure, Trumptee. These are wigs. They're not even gold. They're more orange. Like an orangutan. Are these made from ranga hair?'

'Ain't they delicious?' Trumptee said, patting his wig down on his head. 'Have you ever seen anything more beautiful? They's like a sunset and a sunrise and a crescent moon all rolled into one. Oh, you

can see why I couldn't part with 'em.'
He looked as if he was going to cry.

The Rapunzel

'They're kind of nice, I suppose. Tell us, what's that?' Atticus pushed a couple of wigs aside with the tip of his sword. 'Is it a scroll?'

'Oh, that old thing. That's me map. You can have that. Oh, yeah, there's swords and knives and some Spanish doubloons, too. You can have it all, just let me keep me real treasure. It's not what it's worth, it's what it's worth to me.'

First Mate grabbed the scroll and popped the end off it. 'Oh Captain, my Captain,' he said, 'it's a map, but not like ours. Look. Such detail.' And it was amazing, much more of a

Right comb-over

Left comb-over

The royal wave

The morning glory

Au naturel

map than the one they'd had before. 'Except, there's a rip. It looks like there's a part of it missing.'

The way Captain Trumptee struggled to get away from his reflection in his looking glass was pretty intense.

In an off-handed way, he mumbled, 'Ha harrrrrr! Them other pirates got that bit. Sorry about that. I never kept the map together in case, you know?' He licked a couple of fingers and smoothed his fringe. 'If youse get the other half, it's pretty much everything you'll need to be rich forever. On that, I give you me word as a gentleman, wig-wearing pirate.'

Very gently, he pulled his wigs from the chest, before taking out the doubloons and swords and

knives. They were actually beautiful;
encrusted with sparkling jewels.

Money in the Swear jar

'Junk,' he said, tenderly putting
his wigs back into the chest. 'Now, where's
me quarters? I need me beauty sleep.'

He stood with his chest puffed out, head
back and his lips all puckered up and kissy.

'Hmmmmmm.' Atticus wasn't quite
convinced. He had the map. He had
some treasure. Did he really want Captain
Trumptee as well? 'I've decided to let you
go, Trumptee. You are a prisoner no more.
Stay on your island, with your chest full
of hair.'

'Wouldn't it be fun if he walked the
plank, Captain?' It was Fishface. He
was desperate for someone to do it.

Trumptee protested, saying he
was too scared. It was too dangerous.
'And what about my hair?'

'Bah harrrrrr!' went Fishface.

He went to the end of the plank
and bounced up and down.
'Dangerous? This old thing?' He
did a flip, landing back on the plank.

A chant started. 'Walk the plank. Walk the
plank. Walk the plank.' There was clapping to
go with it. Fishface did another flip, only this
time, when he landed, he bounced twice
as high and dove headfirst into the
water. A cheer went up. 'Walk the
plank. Walk the plank . . .'

'Walk
the
plank'

Muscles moved to Trumptee, who was
backing away like a little dog from a big fight.
'C'mon, Trumptee. It's epic. We do it all
the time.'

'But my treasure . . .'

Atticus closed the lid and locked it,
tossing Trumptee his key. Mullet and Two
Times lowered the chest into the water
with a rope, where it floated perfectly. 'Off
you go, Trumptee. Give Muscles back her

nightshirt. It's time to go – me crew has spoken.'

Trumptee looked around as the crew moved towards him. With his hair treasure safely in the water, he realised there was nothing else for it. He made a run for the plank, bouncing off the end.

'My nightshirt!' bellowed Muscles.

'Mine nooooooooooooooooooooow!' yelled Trumptee before belly-flopping into the water.

'Hate to say it, but he wore it better,' said First Mate to Muscles. 'Now, back to work, squibbers. Aarrrrrr. Get that anchor up, the sails out. We've got treasure to find. Aarrrrrr!'

Chapter 21

The Hunt

The wind freshened as the sun sank lower in the west and within no time they were flying again.

'We'll have that treasure soon enough,' said Mullet, back at the bow of the ship with his arms out.

Soon enough, we'll have it.
And when we do, we'll spend it.
But when it's gone, we'll miss it.
At least we got to get it.

For a night and two days, he sang as *The Grandnan* hammered with the trade winds. Magic Harry kept an eye on the course while

Atticus studied the map.
If only he had the missing
piece, he wouldn't have to
worry about dealing with the horror ship
ahead. Even First Mate was spooked, and
that never seemed to happen.

On the morning of the third day, with
the sun at their backs and the wind on the
wane, Two Times sang out from above. 'Ship
ahooooy! Ship ahoooooy!' Even from the
deck, Atticus could make out the galleon.
Under full sail, she was a sight, all right.

He wondered if they'd seen *The Grandnan* yet.

'Trim the sails,' he said to First Mate. 'Let's catch her by surprise.' When First Mate hesitated, Atticus put out the order himself.

'Trim them sails!'

'But Cap'n, you heard what Trumptee said. She's a viper. They're animals. We don't want to go messing with them.'

Pulling the spyglass from his belt, Atticus laughed. 'Don't you see? That's exactly who we want to go after. If we can take on the ugliest, meanest, most hideous pirates on these seas, we'll be feared forever. There'll be Captain Kidd and Blackbeard, Calico Jack and Madame Cheng. And there'll be me, Atticus Van Tasticus.'

'Don't you want to be a nice pirate, Captain?' said Princess, looking up from the nail she was hammering back into the deck.

'Yeah, don't you want to be liked?' First Mate chimed in.

Atticus thought about it for a second. Then another. 'Well, yeah. Of course. But I don't want to be stomped on, either. This is our chance to get respect. You see? So when they talk about respected pirates, there'll be —'

'Atticus Van Tasticus. I love it!' Hogbreath grinned.

'Hmmmmm, I think I do, too. Trim the sails, aaarrrrrr!' But even with the sails trimmed, *The Grandnan* started to slow. It was the wind – there wasn't quite enough to keep her up on the keel. And once she dropped into the water, she was actually slower than the galleon they were after. 'Aaarrrrrr!' went Atticus.

First Mate was right there with him. 'Maybe it's for the best. I think it might be. Really. Viper, remember?' On the horizon, the galleon was definitely getting smaller.

'She's slipping away, Captain. She's slipping away.'

I'm always right.

He's left me here too long.

'I see that, Two Times.'

'Captain? If I may?' Lightning Rod approached the helm. He'd been doing a lot of thinking and not much talking since the storm. 'Captain, if we were to move the cannons to the back of *The Grandnan* and really load them up – I mean, reaaaaally stuff 'em full of powder – I reckon we could get some kind of a boost out of them. Like, I mean, imagine if we shot 'em all off at once. It'd be like a, I dunno, like some kind of gas propulsion kind of thing. I mean, if you believe Newton and his third law of motion, it should fire *The Grandnan* forwards, shouldn't it?'

For every action there is an equal and opposite reaction

Time to move out. To the apple barrel.

'What magic is this?' said Harry.

'It's physics, Harry.' Lightning Rod looked pretty impressed with himself. 'So, if we fire the cannons, it'll be like

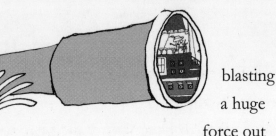

blasting
a huge
force out
the back, which should propel us forwards.
What would you call it? Um. A, um?' Of
course, nobody knew what you might call it
because they couldn't even imagine it.

'Galleon's gone, sir. Galleon's gone.'

'If you think it can work, Rod, do it,' said
Atticus. 'Move the cannons to the stern,
we're going to blast our way forwards. Can
I add one thing to your theory? Balance the
cannons. We have to be careful with this ship,
we don't want to rock it.'

'Aye aye, Captain. Arrrrrr! You heard the
man! Move them cannons!' said Lightning Rod.

It was all hands on deck. The
cannons were rolled out from their
special spots and moved aft. Muscles
made sure they were straight and true.

'Now, stuff 'em full of powder and

let's light 'em up,' went Lightning Rod. He was very animated.

Even though First Mate didn't seem too keen to catch the galleon, there was a fair bit of excitement around firing all the cannons at once.

Lightning Rod had said they all had to be lit at the same time. First Mate thought about Ready, Steady, Go! But these were cannons, not kids. He guessed to light them at the same time, everyone would need more warning.

First Mate had an idea. 'We are going to do a countdown,' he bellowed at the top of his voice. 'On my order, unleash hell! Ten. Nine. Eight. Seven. Six . . .'

Everyone caught on. 'Five. Four. Three. Two . . .'

Ears were covered. Eyes were squinted.

'ONE! Blaaaaast 'em!'

ɔOOOm !

The cinders caught the wicks at exactly the same time, and the five cannons literally erupted.

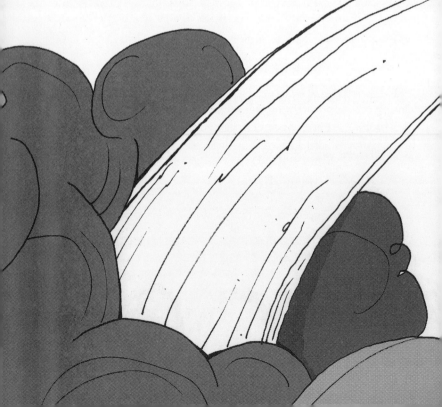

The Grandnan seemed to grumble at first, but then shot forwards, faster than anyone had ever imagined.

And they didn't just get closer to the galleon, they literally caught up.

yahh
hoo

Chapter 22

The Fight

The Grandnan was most definitely a surprise, not that it helped, because the element of surprise was on them as much the galleon. Across the stern in wobbly black letters was her name.

'She's called *Pegasis*, Captain.'

'I'll bet she is,' muttered First Mate to no one in particular. 'Well, duh.'

Muscles, Two Times and Princess were headless because they'd never been into battle before; they had no idea what was going to happen. Mullet and Lightning Rod were buzzing from firing the cannons.

From somewhere aboard *Pegasis* came a deep, manly voice, roaring, 'Prepare to board. Prepare to board. Grappling hooks,

Grrrrrrr

boarding planks, spears, knives and swords at the ready!'

Pegasis was bigger than them. A mighty ship with lots and lots of sailors.

'You might want to think about this for a minute, Cap'n,' said First Mate. 'Your pirate dream could end before it begins. They sound like animals!' He was peeking out from behind Atticus now, trying to get a look at the ship.

Atticus stood firm at the helm, slowly turning *The Grandnan* in towards the enemy ship. 'Whatever they tell their crew to do, we do!' he yelled. 'Boarding planks. Grappling hooks. Spears and knives. Get ready to board!'

The two pirate ships were practically throwing distance apart. Atticus could see there were lots of them, but they weren't so horrible. Not to look at, anyway.

'Baaaargh!' he said.
'Baaaaaarghhhh!'

Baaaaaarghhhh!

#*⊙Ö!*!!

came the blather from the other ship. That
wasn't good. Certainly bad enough for Atticus
to take a step backwards, and First Mate to
shrink even further behind his captain.

'I'm warning you!' came the
call.

It was a strangely familiar
bark, and Atticus wondered how
he could know that voice. It was
coming from behind the bulkhead, as if
hiding for safety. Atticus realised this might
not be the first fight for the other captain.

'This will be a terrible battle,' continued the
familiar voice. 'Like nothing you've ever seen

or imagined. Barrrrrr! Consider your worst, most awful, most bloodiest imaginings, and they will look like a slumber party. You even think about crossing this threshold and it'll be as bad as bad can be.'

'Mmmmmaybe,' whispered First Mate to Atticus.

'There'll be blood and guts and spit and stuff everywhere. I's warning yers!'

Still using Atticus for cover, First Mate offered, 'Nnnnot sure I believe her.'

The sledging from across the water was relentless. 'I've eaten landlubbers like you for breakfast. Squibbers like you for lunch. Baarrrrrr! I had a puppy once for dessert! Your crew will be a snack! Pegasistians, get ready to attack the squibbers!'

First Mate jumped out from behind Atticus. Enough was enough.

I could go a slush puppy.

Caramel dessert.

Is it a boat of whales?

A basket of snails.

A puppy in the desert.

Was that desert or dessert?

Now you're making me hungry.

'Aaaarrrrrr! Bollocks! You have **NEVER** eaten a puppy for dessert!'

The other captain poked her head above the bulkhead. 'I have, too!'

'Peg! You have not!' shouted First Mate. 'Even you wouldn't do that.'

'Peg?' Atticus looked from First Mate to Peg and back again. 'You know her? You actually know her name?'

Everyone stopped what they were doing.

First Mate turned to Atticus and said, 'Well, yeah, kind of. I mean, I should. She is my sister!'

'**Baaaaaaargh!**'

came the cry from the captain of the other ship. 'I'm not just your sister, though, am I?'

Chapter 23

Sister, Sister

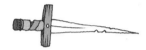

Now everyone froze.

'I'm your twin sister!'

This was unbelievable, like something out of a play. Then, at the top of her voice, Peg shrieked, 'Your IDENTICAL twin sister. And, Gwendolyn, who said you could wear my shoes?'

Gwen?

Gwen?

Did she say 'her umbilical's twisted'?

I think she said 'Your umbrella's twisted.'

No it was 'Weird tentacled skin blister.'

'They're not yours, they're mine. Dad got them for me.'

'Gwendolyn?' Atticus couldn't believe it. None of them could. 'Your name is Gwendolyn?'

'Well, yeah,' said First Mate. 'But it's First Mate to you, 'cos I'm your first mate, remember?'

'And you're a girl?'

There was an echo around *The Grandnan*. 'A girl. She's a she. First Mate's a girl.'

It was First Mate's turn to look surprised. 'I've always been a girl. You knew that, right?'

Atticus raised one eyebrow. Then the other. He looked around at everyone else, who started to nod back at him. 'Yeah. Yeah, I knew. It'd be weird if you were a boy and your name was Gwendolyn, wouldn't it?' Now the crew really nodded. 'We all knew. Duh! It was your *aaaarrrrr*! that gave you away.'

Yeah. yeah.

We know.

Duh. Yep.

First Mate laughed. 'As if.' Then she whispered to Atticus. 'But these *are* her shoes. Don't tell.'

'I heard that,' said Peg. 'I knew it. You're in so much trouble when we get home. Mum and Dad are furious! Your side of our room is a pigsty!'

Atticus bent, pretending to wipe something off the buckle of his boot, and whispered very quietly to First Mate, just to be sure Pirate Peg wouldn't catch on. 'Give her back her shoes for the other half of the treasure map.'

'Good idea, Cap'n. But I bet I know where she's hidden it. I'll make a big fuss and give her the stupid shoes. Then, while I'm making a distraction, you sneak aboard, get the map, sneak back to *The Grandnan* and we'll sail away and be rich as stink. Good plan?' she said in barely a whisper. And then, much louder, she called out, 'All right, Peg. I admit it.

When are we fighting?

When do I get to swing over?

You're right about the shoes. Please let me keep them. *Please*?'

Atticus looked confused. He was pretty sure First Mate – uh, Gwendolyn – had said she'd give them back. She winked at him.

'Never!' barked Pirate Peg. Atticus was beginning to see the viper that Captain Trumptee had been talking about. This girl had bite.

'Ohhhh, Peg! Please,' First Mate whined. 'I won't tell Mum and Dad that you were the one who smashed their special cake plate last Christmas.'

'They know already,' she said. 'Now, toss them shoes over before I blow your ship to smithereens. Cannons. Load the cannons!' Her crew scurried across the deck to the nearside cannons. She was serious.

'They're loading the cannons! They're loading the cannons!' Two Times called from the crow's nest, sounding very uptight. 'Captain?'

'Load our cannons!' yelled First Mate. 'Do it now and do it right! Nice and full. Get 'em ready, we're going into battle!'

Cannons! Load the cannons!

'They're all at the back of the ship, Mate,' whispered Atticus.

'Exactly,' she said, nodding back. 'Load 'em up reaaaaal good!'

The two ships weren't very far apart.

There's another four barrels of powder below.

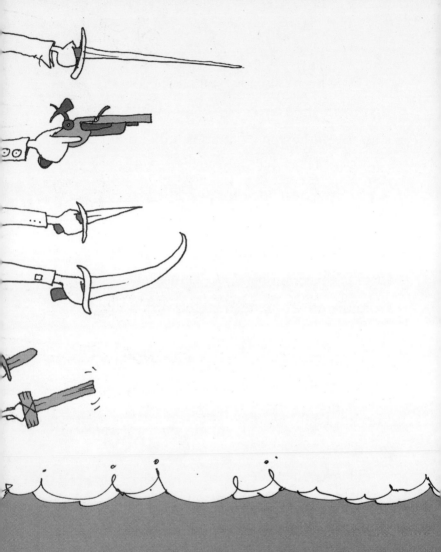

'Just give me my shoes, or else!' went
Pirate Peg.

'Never.'

'Mate!' hissed Atticus. He was properly

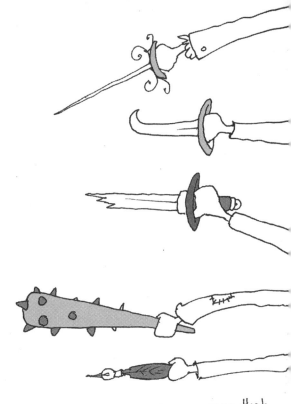

Are you sure that this is mightier than a sword?

worried now. The plan wasn't really working the way he thought it would.

'How're them cannons going?' yelled Peg to her crew. There were lots of 'aye's and 'arrrrr's and a squeaky 'Comin', Captain!'.

Arrrrrrrr

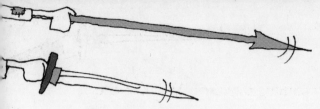

First Mate looked to the stern, where Lightning Rod and Mullet were jamming powder into the final cannon. Once done, they gave her the thumbs up.

'Listen, Peg,' she said, 'what about a swap? Shoes for, say, some treasure?'

Peg was standing on the gunwale of her ship. 'They's my shoes, Gwendolyn. I don't have to swap them for anything! Just give me back my stupid shoes! And because you took them, I'm going to have all your treasure as well.'

The two ships were side by side now and

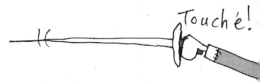
Touché!

very slowly coming together. At worst, they were spearing distance apart.

Atticus curled a finger to First Mate, calling her towards him. 'Mate,' he whispered, 'I've got it. Throw her the shoes. Get the first one on the deck, but toss the second shoe into the bowside net. That's all the distraction I'll need.'

'Brilliant, Cap'n.'

'Mate? Mate? Where will the map be?'

First Mate almost laughed. 'If I know Peg, it'll be under her pillow. Or in a shoebox under her shoes, or, if it's really important to her, in her undies drawer. They're the only places she hides anything.'

Mate? Mate?

'Eeeew,' went Atticus, before counting off the list with his fingers. 'Pillow. Shoebox. Undies drawer. Fingers crossed, eh?' With his index finger to his mouth as a sign for silence, he scampered down to the back of *The Grandnan*, using the gunwale for cover.

First Mate watched him go, and once in position, she hollered at her twin sister.

'Do you have any other shoes, Peg? What about your blue pair with the buckles? I'll trade you them ones!'

'Baarrrrrr! The cannons! Get ready to fire the cannons!' Peg was ferocious.

'**Fine! Fiiiiiine!**'

First Mate yelled back. 'You can have them! Jeeeeez! I'll toss them over. Hey, Peg. Your hair's, like, really frizzy. Did you do that on purpose or have you got split ends? Looks like split ends.'

'I'll give you split ends,' yelled Peg. 'Now, give us me shoes!'

First Mate really took her time taking the shoes off, then walked along the side of *The Grandnan* all the way to the bow of the ship. Everyone watched. There was no talking or yelling, just the creak and groans of two ships swinging distance apart. Atticus used the distraction to launch onto the stern of *Pegasis*, landing like a butterfly with sore feet.

It worked! He couldn't believe it. While First Mate fumbled about doing practice throws, Atticus went below deck, searching for the captain's quarters.

It was easy enough to find. There was a sign on the door saying:

PEG –
Keep Out.
Touch my **STUFF** and you'll be sorry.
Specially
NOT my shoes
#G 🦴 !!

On deck

First Mate's first throw was a beauty. Pirate
Peg caught her shoe and inspected it. 'Did
you look after them at *all*?' she said, sounding
a little sad. First Mate lined up for the second
throw.

Below deck

With fingers crossed, Atticus raised the pillow
on the bed. There was nothing there. *Humph!*
he thought. *That's a shame.* He found the
wardrobe and figured the set-up would be the
same for everyone – socks and jocks at the top.

Shirts, shorts, pants down the bottom. There was a closet for hanging things up, too, with shoes lined up at the bottom. There were shoeboxes under the shoes. With shoes in them, mostly. And at the very bottom in the hardest to reach corner was one last, skanky looking box.

He almost didn't bother with it.

On deck

'Ready. Steady. Oh, hang on. Sorry, nearly slipped,' went First Mate.

Pirate Peg looked ready to thrash her. 'Oh, COME ON!'

'Ready, steady . . .' First Mate tossed the shoe. It was a terrible throw. Totally hopeless but absolutely perfect in the way it

What weapon is this?

A double-barrelled catapult?

bounced off the side of *Pegasis* and landed in the net used for the ship's extra storage.

'Whoopsie!' went First Mate. 'Soz about that. It's okay, though. I can see it. It's just hanging on there almost like it's going to fall through the hole and into the ocean, where it'll sink and never be seen again. Oh well. If you get attacked by a whale or a shark, make sure you lose your left leg, Peg. Then you can use the shoe you've got. Uh-huh!'

No one had ever heard her sound so light and breezy.

'Don't touch it!

DOOOOON'T GO NEAR THAT SHOE WITH A POOOOOLE!'

roared Peg.

'DO NOT DROP THAT SHOE IN THE OCEEEEEEAN!'

Below deck

Treasure maps! Not just one, but heaps of them! Atticus Van Tasticus had hit the mother lode of treasure maps, all in that manky old box at the back of the closet. He picked it up, tucked it under his arm and got ready to bolt. It was amazing. There'd be loot for years in this one shoebox. He was so excited he nearly squealed.

Almost out the door, he stopped and looked at the wardrobe. If something this valuable was hidden in the shoebox, he wondered what could be under the undies.

He didn't want to look, but then . . . he kind of had to.

With the shoebox under this arm, Atticus tiptoed back to the chest of drawers. The top drawer was sticky, so he had to rattle and jiggle it. Setting the shoebox on the floor, he worked a little harder to open the drawer. *Soap*, he thought.

Shhhh!
Follow me.

She needs to rub soap on the edges to make it work better. He jiggled and he pulled, and very slowly, the drawer gave way.

On deck

Almost the entire crew of *Pegasis* was stretched out, hand to foot to hand to foot in a giant, human ladder stretching all the way down to the net holding the shoe.

'Don't shake that net,' said Peg. The fear in her voice was very real as she climbed her way down. 'Don't drop that shoe.'

First Mate watched on. It was hilarious. All this over a shoe! She'd told Princess to

keep an eye aft, and as soon as Atticus was
back on board, she wanted to know.

'Nearly there. Nearly there,' yelled Two
Times from the crow's nest.

'I know. I know,' Pirate Peg yelled back.
'Steady, I've almost got it.' Her hand reached
out. She really was nearly there!

First Mate gave Mullet and Lightning
Rod a very small thumbs up. The crew of
The Grandnan were ready.

Below deck

'Come on. Come on . . .' The drawer finally
opened. Socks to the left, undies to the right.
'Socks first. Please be under the socks.'

Atticus slid his hands in and searched under

the left-hand side, but there was nothing, just a
bit of sand. Trying not to think too much, he
fished around under the undies. 'If this is the
most special spot, there has to be something,
Pirate Peg. What is it?' There was nothing
but a bit of drawer lining. *Unless, hang on*, he
thought. *What if it's not drawer lining?*

His heart nearly stopped. Maybe it was the
famous *Map of Maps – the Mother of Them All.*

Could it be? Very carefully, Atticus pulled the paper out. He couldn't have been more surprised.

On deck

'Got it. I've got it.' Peg tucked the shoe into her waistband and said, 'Pull me up. I've got the shoe. Pull me up.' She huffed and puffed as the human ladder retreated. 'Now you're going to really get it, Gwendolyn,' she hissed.

'This time you've really, really done it.'

This
time
you've
really
done
it!

Below deck

It was beautiful. An artwork, in fact. Atticus could see the value in it straightaway. It was priceless – worth more than money. In his hand was the most perfect portrait of

First Mate and Pirate Peg together. Smiling. Twinkling. Party dresses and spirally hair. He gently set it back under the undies and pushed the drawer closed as best he could.

'Nice,' he said, before grabbing the shoebox, racing out of the cabin, up the back steps and out onto the deck.

It was a short climb up the ladder to the swinging rope and he was through the air and onto *The Grandnan* before Pirate Peg was back on the gunwale, catching her breath.

'He's back!' Princess signaled to First Mate. 'Atticus Van Tasticus is back!' She sounded so happy.

First Mate cleared her throat and let out an *aaaaarrrrrr*! She jumped up on the gunwale and was literally swiping distance from her sister. Seeing the two of them so close made it obvious how identical they really were.

'So good to see you, my favourite twin sister.' First Mate smiled. 'Alas, it is time to bid farewell. On my order!' she called to the back of the ship. 'Cannons!'

'Noooooooo,' yelped Peg, jumping down onto the deck. 'Gwen, NO! You can't, Gwen. You can't!'

'Goodbye, sister,' said First Mate. 'Farewell.'

Before she'd even ordered for the cannons to be fired, the entire crew of *Pegasis* had taken cover. To be fired on at such close range would surely be a catastrophe.

'On my order!

Five,
Four,
Three —

Did you hear her say 'fire'?

I think someone said 'moo'.

'Noooooo, Gwenny. No!'

Atticus and the crew joined the count.

'Two, One, Fiiiiiiiire!'

There was a hiss and crackle as flint touched wick, and with Peg's pirate crew under cover, the cannons aboard *The Grandnan* exploded as one.

POW

It was like thunder in your guts, then
fire and smoke and waves and whoosh.
The Grandnan took off.

Chapter 24

Another New Plan

The gentle splash and slap of water against the bow was like an anthem. The sun was up, the wind was down and, apart from a few snorting dolphins, there was nothing but *The Grandnan* under half sail on an ocean of possibility.

'Did you find the other half of the map yet, Harry?' said Atticus, using a fishbone to clean the gaps in his teeth.

'Maybe,' said Harry. 'There's a stack of half maps here. I'm sure it has to be one of them.' He'd been at it for a while now, trying to match up their half of Trumptee's map with one of the maps from Pirate Peg's shoebox. 'If it's here, I'll find it.'

'Indeed you will,' said Atticus. He'd made a long steerer out of ropes and sat at the back of *The Grandnan*, completely relaxed.

First Mate sat next to him and didn't speak for the longest time. But she had to ask. 'Cap'n, did you happen to look in her undies drawer? Just in case?'

Atticus smiled. 'Well, to be honest –'

'Ship ahoy, Captain! Ship ahoy!'

Two Times belted it out from the crow's nest. 'Tell me that's not that galleon *Pegasis*, Captain. Please. Tell me that's not *Pegasis*.'

Eie-eee-ee-eeeee-eehee.

Hoist the Jolly Roger, sharpen yer cutlass and load the cannons — 'tis time fer ye to embrace yer inner pirate!

Place one o' the options below between yer first and last names and ye'll be an official pirate. Aarrrr!

Ivory Bones
Fishface
Slapfoot
Sly Dog
Ugly Mug
Hogbreath
Scallywag
Blue Mane
Silverbeard
Stinkeye

Scurvy Sailor
Mad Dog
McGhostface
Magic Harry
Van Tasticus
Coconut
Crazy
One-Legged
Knee Biter
Scoundrel

Why call me Fishface?

How to draw

Atticus Van Tasticus

WHAT YOU NEED

❊ 2B (or similar) pencil.
❊ Black (felt tip) pen.
❊ A scribbly mind.

Use your pencil to begin.
Think of Atticus as being made from
a bunch of shapes: circles, ovals, triangles and lines.
As you improve, be more scribbly and free.
He's an action character, so the faster
you draw the more energy he'll have.

Details like hands can also be easy if thought of as simple shapes: a circle for a fist or the palm. If you need fingers, draw sausages. Feet are triangles with scribbly circles for toes. Inside toes are bigger than outside toes.

This is a quick two-stage, scribbly rough.

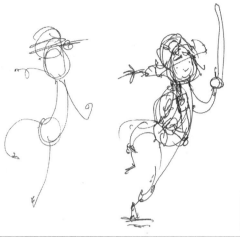

A pirate parrot is the letter "B" tilted with a curved triangle shape, plus added details.

Think of Attiucus's hat like it's made from folded paper. Simply add some curves later. The skull and crossed bones is an oval with two rectangles. Draw a scribbly 'X' over the top to make sure the bones line up on the opposite side.

TO FINISH

☠ Place a new piece of paper over your scribbly drawing.

☠ Trace through using your black pen for a clean, finished and ready-for-action . . .

Aaaaaarrr!

Whichever way Atticus is looking, his hat always faces forward.

Atticus Van Tasticus